MW01048352

Stories

in the shape

of ...

Pierre W H S Gilbert

Wasteland Press
www.wastelandpress.net
Shelbyville, KY USA

Stories in the Shape of...
by Pierre W H S Gilbert

First Printing – October 2012
ISBN: 978-1-60047-789-8

Editing: Susan Giffin
sgawritestuff@yahoo.com

Photography: Wade P. Streeter
www.openlakegroup.com

Printed in the U.S.A.

0   1   2   3   4   5   6

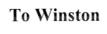

To Winston

Stories in the Shape of...

A STORY IN THE SHAPE OF

a stage play

AN ORDINARY DAY

INT. AN APARTMENT. THE STAGE. LIT.

IN THE BACK OF THE STAGE, A WALL, BLANK, WHITE. IN THE CENTER OF THAT WHITE WALL: A DOOR, SPECIAL, IMPORTANT, BAROQUE, ROCOCO, HOLLYWOOD-LIKE PLASTER FROM THE THIRTIES, CONTRASTING WITH THE BANALITY OF THE REST OF THE APARTMENT. THE DOOR OPENS TO THE OUTSIDE WORLD. OVER THE DOOR IS A BIG SQUARE, 3 FEET BY 3 FEET, BLACK, BLANK, LIKE THE SCREEN OF AN ALARM CLOCK LEFT UNPLUGGED.

TOWARD THE FRONT OF THE STAGE:

ON THE LEFT, A PIECE OF WALL AT A 30-DEGREE ANGLE FROM THE CORNER OF THE STAGE. AGAINST THAT PIECE OF WALL ON A LONG NARROW TABLE ARE ALL KINDS OF BOTTLES FULL OF PILLS. NEXT TO THE TABLE, AN ARMCHAIR, COMFORTABLE BUT OBVIOUSLY TIRED, USED FOR MANY, MANY YEARS.

ON THE RIGHT, ANOTHER PIECE OF WALL, AT A 30-DEGREE ANGLE FROM THE CORNER OF THE STAGE, PLACED SYMMETRICALLY TO THE ONE ON THE LEFT BUT LEAVING A PATH TO THE RIGHT FOR A PERSON OR TWO. IN FRONT OF THAT PIECE OF WALL, A MATTRESS, COVERED WITH A BLANKET HELD TO A TOP SHEET WITH CLOTHESPINS. AND A PILLOW IN A PILLOWCASE. THE TOP SHEET, THE BOTTOM SHEET, AND THE

PILLOWCASE ARE MISMATCHED. ON THE FLOOR NEXT
TO THE MATTRESS ARE A FEW SHALLOW BOWLS.

THOSE TWO PIECES OF WALL ARE COVERED WITH
YELLOWED WALLPAPER AND A FEW FRAMED PRINTS.

> The lights are abruptly turned off. The
> curtain falls. With the hall pitch-black, the
> curtain rises.

> SCENE 1

> The stage is dark. But on the mattress, one
> gets a glimpse at, one guesses, a human
> form. Over the back door, a big 1 in bright
> neon color in the black screen.

JEANNE (O.S.)
(strong and cheerful voice)
Come on, get up, everybody! Time to get out of bed!

> Exactly at the same time, lights on the stage.
> A naked man, GERARD, age to be
> determined by the director, his legs stuck to
> each other, and his arms stuck to his body,
> laughs.

GERARD
You make me laugh with that every day.

> JEANNE walks on stage. Age to be
> determined by the director. Semi-elegant.
> Robe/kimono with pink feathers at the neck
> and wrists. High heel mules with pink
> pompoms.

JEANNE
(walking toward Gérard)
Did you have a good night sleep, my love? Look at you. Your blanket is on the floor! You didn't get cold, I hope.

GERARD
A little bit. No big deal.

JEANNE
You should have called me.

GERARD
And wake you up?

JEANNE
Why not?

GERARD
I'm OK.

She picks the blanket and sheet and covers him.

JEANNE
Is it better, now?

GERARD
Yes, it is better.

JEANNE
I should buy you a sleeping bag.

GERARD
(visibly agitated)
Never! I would feel trapped.

JEANNE
But you wouldn't be cold anymore.

GERARD

Never!

JEANNE

As you wish! I'm gonna go make some coffee.

> She tickles his nose with the pompom of her mule.

GERARD
(laughing)

Stop, you're tickling me!

JEANNE
(jokingly sulking)

You don't like it?

> She tickles his nose again with the pompom of her mule. He laughs again.

JEANNE
(teasing him)

You want me to stop?

GERARD

Yes and no, you know that. Go make the coffee!

JEANNE

Yes, my sweet, beloved husband.

> She disappears into what is the kitchen that we don't see. We hear kitchen noises. Both Jeanne and Gérard speak louder to be heard by each other.

GERARD

What are you gonna do today?

JEANNE (O.S.)
(from the kitchen)
Nothing special. Grocery shopping, the laundry. And probably a soup.

GERARD
You and your soups!

JEANNE (O.S.)
(teasingly sulky tone)
You don't like my soups?

GERARD
You know I adore them.

JEANNE (O.S.)
Liar!

GERARD
And on Sundays, you call them your eurosoups!

JEANNE (O.S.)
So what, if it's Sunday...

GERARD
And also, it's easier to eat with a spoon.

JEANNE (O.S.)
Yes, but I also cut your other food into tiny pieces. You can't just eat soup, over and over again.

GERARD
I really prefer soup. And mashed potatoes.

JEANNE (O.S.)
But, with your mashed potatoes, you need some meat and vegetables.

GERARD

Not really.

JEANNE (O.S.)

Of course, you do. For the proteins, the vitamins, and the minerals.
Everybody knows that!

GERARD
(sounding uninterested and bored, rolling his eyes)

I suppose!

> Jeanne reappears from the kitchen, holding a
> shallow bowl in her hand.

JEANNE

Your coffee is served, my Lord.

> She kneels in front of him. He slowly turns
> to his side. She brings the bowl to his lips.

JEANNE

Tell me if it's too hot.

> He has a sip.

GERARD

It is perfect. You make such wonderful coffee.

JEANNE

Coffee is coffee.

GERARD

You know it is not true. You've always hated compliments.

JEANNE

Compliments make me uncomfortable, you know that.

GERARD

Even when I tell you that you are the most beautiful woman in the world?

JEANNE

Specially when you drink your coffee. It's getting cold.

GERARD

If you have to, you'll make me a fresh cup, or rather a fresh bowl, like for a dog.

JEANNE

Stop it!

GERARD

I'm sorry.

JEANNE

Finish your coffee. I'll bring you your yogurt. With pieces of fresh pineapple.

GERARD

My favorite! But first, dance for me, please.

JEANNE

Finish your coffee!

> He finishes his coffee. She takes a paper napkin from the pocket of her robe and wipes his mouth.

JEANNE

I'll dance after the yogurt. It will be your dessert.

GERARD

You are mean to make me wait until then.

JEANNE

I am a sadist.

>She gets up. Takes the bowl back to the
kitchen. Comes back with a bowl and a
spoon: the yogurt. She starts to kneel again
but...

JEANNE

Your vitamins! I almost forgot your vitamins! And of course, you
don't say anything!

>She puts the bowl on the floor, goes to the
medicine table, and starts opening some
bottles and putting the vitamins together.
Meanwhile:

GERARD
(making faces)
Vitamins! Fartamins! Pissamins! Shitamins!

JEANNE

Stop acting like a spoiled child!

GERARD

But I am spoiled: I have you.

>She puts the vitamins in her hand and comes
back toward him. Kneels again. Fills the
spoon with yogurt, puts the vitamins in it.

JEANNE

The yogurt will make them slide.

GERARD

For what they do!

JEANNE

The doctor said that it is very important that...

GERARD
(making clown faces)

The dooooooooooooooooooooooooctor!

JEANNE

If you want me to dance, you will have to shut up and eat your yogurt with the V-I-T-A-M-I-N-S!!

GERARD

Yogurt, yogurt! Quick, quick! And vitamins too! Quick, quick!

JEANNE

What's wrong with you today? It must be the full moon!

> She feeds him the yogurt, a spoonful at a time.

JEANNE

There, it's almost done. Wasn't it good?

GERARD

Yum-yum! Good the yogurt! Good the yogurt! Yum-yum!

JEANNE

You're out of your mind today!

> She wipes his mouth again with the paper napkin, gets up, and takes the bowl back to the kitchen.

GERARD
(very loud and very show businesslike)

And now, ladies and gentlemen, the moment we all have been waiting for: from Paris, Madame Jeanne and her new ballet: the Dancing Goddess!

He turns around with great difficulty, so that he has a better view of her dancing.

GERARD
(obviously unable to applaud)
Bravo! Bravo! Bravo!

Jeanne walks in, holding a cheap CD player in her hand, and puts it on the table next to the vitamins bottles. She turns it on.
(note: I really liked the scene in "The Bride Wore Black" where Jeanne Moreau dances on a mandolin concerto by, I believe, Vivaldi. Something similar would be better than a pop song. Gluck? Satie? Also, it should be acted in a very respectful manner, not at all like a caricature.)

She starts to dance, very sensual. They start to flirt. She dances, they flirt. She dances, they flirt. Jeanne stops dancing at the exact moment the music stops, in a very professional manner.

GERARD
Bravo! Bravo! Bravo!

JEANNE
(smiling)
You liked it?

GERARD
You were fabulous.

JEANNE
You always say that.

GERARD
But it's so true.

> She gets close to him and tickles his nose
> with the pompom of her mule again. He
> laughs.

JEANNE

I'm gonna go get ready now. Think about things you need.

GERARD

A pair of pants!

> They laugh. She disappears behind the wall
> and goes to the bedroom to get dressed.

JEANNE (O.S.)

You want me to bring you the TV?

GERARD

Absolutely not! I hate TV, you know that.

JEANNE (O.S.)

I don't like for you to be like that, in the silence.

GERARD

It relaxes me.

JEANNE (O.S.)

It would get me depressed.

GERARD

Buy some chocolate ice cream. I feel like it.

> Jeanne walks back into the room. Chanel-ish
> suit, string of pearls, bracelets, high heels.

GERARD

Let me look at you!

JEANNE
(ignoring his remark)
What's the weather like?

She goes to the door in the back of the stage.
Opens it. Blue sky, dazzling. Fake like a
postcard.

JEANNE
No need for a raincoat today! Come and look!

He crawls toward the door.

GERARD
Yes.

She's looking at him.

JEANNE
I would like to talk to you about something. It means a lot to me.

He doesn't say anything, but you can feel
the fear. She closes the door.

JEANNE
I met the neighbor the other day...

He becomes tense.

JEANNE
A delightful young man. Beefy guy. I told him about you.

GERARD
(sarcastic)
Really?

JEANNE
About our situation...

GERARD

Why? It's nobody's business.

JEANNE

(talking very fast, so Gérard can't interrupt her)

He told me that he would help me put you in a wheelchair so we could go for a walk together.

GERARD

(furious)

But I have no interest in going for a walk. A walk indeed!

(laughing viciously)

In that pollution! And all that noise! You should have talked to me about it before...

JEANNE

So that you would tell me exactly that!

GERARD

I'm fine here. It's my refuge, my kingdom.

JEANNE

But it would do you good to get out, to get some fresh air. You haven't left this place since, since...

GERARD

Say it, come on, say it.

JEANNE

Please calm down! It was just an idea. Because, by myself, I couldn't do it. But for him, it's nothing.

GERARD

So, you must have had some long conversations, you and Mister Muscles.

JEANNE

But what are you talking about? He's willing to help me; that's all.

GERARD

Oh, I'm sure of that!

JEANNE

To help us. What's wrong with you?

GERARD

That's what it was for, the suit, the pearls, and the high heels.

JEANNE

You are crazy. Stop! Anyway, I'm tired of listening to your bullshit. Stay in your hole for the rest of your life if it's what you want.

> As soon as she says that, she gets on her knees in front of him.

JEANNE

Forgive me. You know I didn't mean it.

> She kisses him on the forehead, caresses his cheek. He doesn't show any emotion. She gets up and walks to the door.

JEANNE

My bag!

> She goes to the bedroom, comes back with her bag. She looks at Gérard. Still no emotion on his face. She walks toward the door. Tense silence.

GERARD

And where does he come from, that neighbor?

JEANNE

From next door, believe it or not!

GERARD

You never told me about him.

JEANNE

He just moved in a week ago.

GERARD

To the left or to the right?

> She sits down in the armchair, takes her
> shoes off, unbuttons her jacket.

JEANNE

To the right.

GERARD

To the right, it's Mrs. Durant.

JEANNE

It's her son. He inherited the house.

GERARD

Mrs. Durant is dead?

JEANNE

Of course. She died three months ago.

GERARD

And you didn't tell me?

JEANNE

I probably forgot.

GERARD

Forgot!!!!! And what else did you forget to tell me? That we are at war with Liechtenstein?

JEANNE
Yes, we are at war with Liechtenstein. If you watched TV or
listened to the radio, you would know that!

GERARD
Very funny, Jeanne. And I suppose that they also announced Mrs.
Durant's death on the radio and on TV.

JEANNE
Anyway, you didn't like her.

GERARD
And neither did you. You much prefer her son, the muscle man.
And what does that person do for a living, may I ask?

JEANNE
I have no idea. We didn't talk about that.

GERARD
(imitating her with a nasty tone)
I have no idea. We didn't talk about that.

> She puts her shoes back on, re-buttons her
> jacket, and grabs her bag. She goes toward
> the back door.

JEANNE
You're really too stupid. I'm going to go spend some money. I'm
asking one last time: Do you need anything?

GERARD
To be left alone.

> She opens the door, leaves, slams it. Long
> silence. Gérard turns around and gets ready
> to go back to bed, then stops.

The curtain falls. The curtain rises a few minutes later.

SCENE 2

The set is exactly the same as for the first part, except that over the back door is now a number 2.

Jeanne is next to the back door, Gérard is on the floor. The beginning is played EXACTLY like the first time.

GERARD

So, you must have had some long conversations, you and Mister Muscles.

JEANNE

But what are you talking about? He's willing to help me; that's all.

GERARD

Oh, I'm sure of that!

JEANNE

To help us. What's wrong with you?

GERARD

That's what it was for, the suit, the pearls, and the high heels.

JEANNE

You are crazy. Stop! Anyway, I'm tired of listening to your bullshit. Stay in your hole for the rest of your life if it's what you want.

As soon as she says that, she gets on her knees in front of him.

JEANNE

Forgive me. You know I didn't mean it.

> She kisses him on the forehead, caresses his cheek. He doesn't show any emotion. She gets up and walks towards the door.

JEANNE

My bag!

> She goes to the bedroom, comes back with her bag. She looks at Gérard. Still no emotion on his face. She walks toward the door. Tense silence.

GERARD

And where does he come from, that neighbor?

JEANNE

From next door, believe it or not!

GERARD

You never told me about him.

JEANNE

He just moved in a week ago.

GERARD

To the left or to the right?

> She sits down in the armchair, takes her shoes off, unbuttons her jacket.

JEANNE

To the right.

GERARD

To the right, it's Mrs. Durant.

JEANNE

It's her son. He inherited the house.

GERARD

Mrs. Durant is dead?

JEANNE

Of course. She died three months ago.

GERARD

And you didn't tell me?

JEANNE

I probably forgot.

GERARD

Forgot!!!!! And what else did you forget to tell me? That we are at war with Liechtenstein?

JEANNE

Yes, we are at war with Liechtenstein. If you watched TV or listened to the radio, you would know that!

GERARD

Very funny, Jeanne. And I suppose that they also announced Mrs. Durant's death on the radio and on TV.

JEANNE

Anyway, you didn't like her.

GERARD

And neither did you. You prefer her son, the muscle man. And what does that person do for a living, may I ask?

JEANNE

I have no idea. We didn't talk about that.

GERARD
(imitating her with a nasty tone)

I have no idea. We didn't talk about that.

> She puts her shoes back on, re-buttons her
> jacket and grabs her bag. She gets up and
> goes toward the back door.

JEANNE

You're really too stupid. I'm going to go spend some money. I'm asking one last time: Do you need anything?

GERARD

To be left alone.

> She opens the door, leaves, slams it. Long
> silence. Gérard turns around and gets ready
> to go back to bed, then stops.

GERARD

She went to meet him, I'm sure! That's why she's wearing her Sunday suit! And the pearls! Even though they're fake!
(sticks his tongue out)
It was for him! Certainly not for me! And she was in such a hurry to leave! I must find out!

> He crawls toward the back door as fast as he
> can, looks for an opening so he can look
> outside.

GERARD

There must be a crack, a hole, a space. I'm sure. I can feel the air come in when it's cold. Where is it?

> He gets as close as possible to the door and
> starts inspecting it. At that very moment, the

door opens and bangs Gérard's head and
pushes him a few inches back.

JEANNE (O.S.)
(exasperated)
But what's going on? The door is stuck, now?

She closes the door and reopens it
vigorously, banging it again on Gérard's
head.

GERARD
Stop! Let me move!

JEANNE
What's happening? You're driving me crazy!

She closes the door.

GERARD
(screams)
Noooooooooooooo!

Jeanne reopens the door, banging Gérard's
head again.

JEANNE
Don't be afraid. I'm coming!

Gérard moves away from the door as fast as
he can.

JEANNE
This time is the one.

Jeanne reopens the door. Gérard barely
escapes it.

JEANNE

I'm gonna have to oil that door. Frankly, there is always something that needs to be done!

GERARD

Gérard, hurt!

JEANNE

What is it?

GERARD

What is it? You banged the door on my head three times! I'm probably gonna have a bump. I have such a headache!

JEANNE

Frankly, what were you doing at the door? Doors get opened, you know!

GERARD

You were gone shopping!

JEANNE

I forgot my wallet. I changed bags. That why I came back. Poor baby, go lie down. I'll bring you an aspirin.

> He goes to his bed, lies down while she goes to the kitchen to put water in a bowl. She comes back, puts the bowl on the table with the medicine bottles and looks for aspirin. She doesn't look at Gérard the whole time she talks to him. He's in terrible pain.

JEANNE

How are you feeling? But where are those aspirin? And your headache? Between the two of us, we really take a lot of medication! Are you feeling better? I was sure we had some aspirin. Try to relax! I wonder if I took them to the kitchen. But no, why would have I done that? Try to take a nap. In the bedroom? No, I'm sure not. I always keep all the medications here. Always.

So that I would always find them, precisely! I don't understand!
Aspirin, really, I always have a bottle. You're feeling better? I'm
gonna go to the neighbor and ask him for a few.

GERARD
(jealously)
It's not necessary. I feel much better. I don't need aspirin.

JEANNE
I wonder if they fell under the table, by any chance.

She leans over, looks under the table.

JEANNE
No. I can't understand. Stay where you are! Don't go glue yourself
to the door! I'll be back in two minutes.

GERARD
I'm telling you: I'm fine.

JEANNE
You don't want me to go to the neighbor, is it what it is?

GERARD
But no.

JEANNE
But, yes, that's what it is.

She laughs. Finally turns to him.

JEANNE
And so, my man is jealous!

GERARD
Not at all. Really, not at all!

She goes to his bed, kneels.

JEANNE

Where does it hurt?

GERARD

On the top, on the right, on the back.

> She puts her lips where she thinks it is.

JEANNE

There?

GERARD

A little lower.

> She puts her lips where he says it is.

JEANNE

It's better now?

GERARD

Much better. No more need for aspirin now!

JEANNE

Well, I cannot live without aspirin in the house. I'm going to the drugstore!

GERARD

No reason to.

> She doesn't listen to him. Grabs her bag and leaves. Closes the door.

GERARD

She was in such a rush! Something is going on!

> He goes back to the door, looks for the crack, the hole.

JEANNE (O.S.)
(at the door)

My wallet!

GERARD

Noooooooooooooooooooo!

The light is turned off at once. The curtain
falls. The curtain rises a few minutes later.

SCENE 3

The set is exactly the same as for the first
part, except that over the back door is now a
number 3. The beginning is played
EXACTLY like the first time.

Jeanne is sitting in the armchair. She puts
her shoes back on, re-buttons her jacket and
grabs her bag. She gets up and goes toward
the back door.

JEANNE

You're really too stupid. I'm going to go spend some money. I'm
asking one last time: Do you need anything?

GERARD

To be left alone.

She opens the door, leaves, slams it. Long
silence. Gérard turns around and gets ready
to go back to bed, then stops.

GERARD

Alone at last. Quiet, without anybody. Just slowly dying.

He goes to the bed, gets in it, grabs the
pillowcase with his mouth, and moves it a
little bit.

                    GERARD
Perfect happiness!

He hums a song, finds the right spot, tries to
fall asleep.

                    GERARD
I hope she doesn't forget the chocolate ice cream. I wonder what
kind of soup she's gonna come up with.

He looks at the floor, inspects it. He gets out
of his bed, crawls to the armchair, looks
under it and under the table.

                    GERARD
It's time for her to run the vacuum. It's a good thing I'm not
allergic to dust.
                    (laughing)
I'd be dead!

He goes back to the bed. Gets in it.

                    GERARD
I'm bored! She certainly takes her time! For a couple of potatoes
and some ice cream. I'm bored! How I miss reading a book,
turning the pages of a magazine.

The door opens a touch.

                    JEANNE (O.S.)
Gérard, my love, are you presentable? We have a visitor. Isabelle
is here.

GERARD
(muttering)

Not Isabelle!

> He gets out of the bed and hides behind the
> wall next to his bed. Jeanne and Isabelle
> come in. Jeanne is holding a cake box. She
> goes to the kitchen to hide it and comes
> back. She goes to Gérard's bed.

JEANNE

Gérard, where are you? I know you're here. Don't hide! Come and
say hi to Isabelle!

> Gérard sheepishly comes out from behind
> the wall. Isabelle sits down in the armchair.

GERARD

Good morning, Isabelle, how are you doing?

> He gets back in bed.

ISABELLE

Like usual, so-so. And you?

GERARD

Oh, you know, same old, same old.

> They have nothing to say to each other, and
> that's obvious. Silence. Jeanne arrives with a
> birthday cake on a platter. A single candle.

JEANNE

Happy birthday, my beloved Gérard!

GERARD

My birthday! I had forgotten.

ISABELLE
(to say something)
What a beautiful cake!

JEANNE
I'm gonna go slice it. It's super chocolate. My husband adores
chocolate.

ISABELLE
Me too.

Jeanne goes back to the kitchen. Isabelle and
Gérard look at each other with a stupid look.

GERARD
And how is Alain?

ISABELLE
I threw him out!

Gérard doesn't know what to say and
therefore doesn't say anything. Jeanne
comes in with two plates full of cake. She
gives one to Isabelle, and brings the other,
which has the lit candle, to Gérard. She
kneels in front of Gérard.

JEANNE
Go ahead, birthday boy, blow it!

Everybody sings: Happy birthday! He blows
the candle out. Jeanne uses a spoon to give
Gérard his cake.

ISABELLE
The cake is really delicious! Chocolate, chocolate, chocolate! I
adore chocolate! Did you see the hunk who just moved next door
to you? A real porn star!

> Gérard freezes. Jeanne doesn't know what to
> do with the cake. She puts the plate down on
> the floor near the bed.

GERARD

Have you met that young man?

> He looks at Jeanne. If looks could kill!

ISABELLE

He is not shy, I can tell you that! And he knows how to seduce women! But he's gorgeous. And full of muscles. Haven't you met him?

JEANNE

We have said hi to each other.

> She looks at Gérard.

JEANNE

We are neighbors, after all.

> Jeanne goes to the kitchen and opens a bottle
> of champagne. The cork pops.
>
> From then on, the 3 actors recite their texts
> independently of each other. And it becomes
> a NON-CONVERSATION where the texts
> are unrelated to each other. Isabelle stays in
> the armchair, Gérard on his bed, and Jeanne
> comes and goes between the kitchen and the
> room, from time to time, holding a glass of
> champagne in her hand. At one point, she
> brings a piece of cake to Isabelle. The
> director and the actors intertwine these
> monologues as they feel.

ISABELLE

Even though, muscles, muscles, muscles, That's not enough!
Personally I find hairy men super sexy. Especially on the back
which, in general, is considered non-civilized. What a crazy idea!
It's brainwashing! And on the shoulders. Everywhere! When I get
fucked, I love to hold on to a hairy back or, like I say, a furry back.
Even though, fur, fur, fur, that's not the only thing. The eyes, the
nose. Some men have such a beautiful nose. And the ears. And the
hands. Everything. It depends, from one man to the next. And then
there is tenderness, of course, and faithfulness. Faithfulness is so
important. Alain? I threw him out because of that. He was
constantly seducing other women with his inviting looks, probably
like your new neighbor does. This cake is delicious.

Jeanne brings her a fresh piece of cake.

ISABELLE

Thank you, Jeanne. I could feed myself with cake and nothing else.
But I must be careful. I gain weight very easily. You know? For
me to have the perfect man, I would have to make him myself, like
the Frankenstein creature. In a Gothic chateau, surrounded by
hairy, muscled peasants who love opera: the best! And another
thing: Men who cry listening to Maria Callas make me melt.
Unfortunately for my butt, most of them are gay.

So, in Frankenstein's castle, I would take the biceps of one, the
brain of another one, the sex of a third one. But I'm dreaming.
Nobody is perfect, not even made up monsters. And robots? It's
not gonna happen overnight! This cake is so good. Shit, I can feel
it going straight to my butt. Anyway, we have to satisfy ourselves
with a human man. That's life. No Frankenstein's monster.

JEANNE

Of course, I've met him. On my way to the grocery store. It's
obvious, he lives next door. He's very attractive, and he's pleasant.
I wonder what his father looked like because, frankly, I would
never have guessed that he was Mrs. Durant's son. Gérard, was
Mr. Durant still alive when we moved here? I don't remember. It's
true that for a reason or another, we never liked Mrs. Durant.

Especially you. I wonder why. Well, it's not important anymore; she's dead. But we have to eat. Honestly, however, there are days when, if I didn't force myself, I would just open a can. Because, frankly, I'm tired of soup. I'm fed up with soup. Tomato soup. Leek soup. This and that soup. Soup, always soup. And mashed potatoes, mashed potatoes. This champagne is not bad at all. I'll just have another sip. It doesn't happen every day. And the cake isn't bad, either. I should buy one more often. It doesn't have to be a birthday.

GERARD

It's my birthday, but I suppose I'm on a diet. Isabelle is stuffing herself with cake, and Jeanne is getting drunk in the kitchen. It's wonderful. I should fart and break the charm. I would like some champagne! By any chance, could I have a little bowl of champagne before you finish the bottle? Nothing from the kitchen! I suppose that getting drunk, just like masturbation, makes you deaf. And that cake is tempting me. Well, since nobody is paying any attention to me, frankly, I don't see why I should give a shit!

> He puts his face to the plate and starts eating the piece of cake. He's got cake all over his face, and he pigs out. He finishes the cake. He licks his lips.

GERARD

DE-LI-CI-OUS. A little bowl of champagne would make it slide, but since the waitress is busy, a sip of water will have to do.

> He crawls to a bowl next to the bed and has a sip. The light is turned off at once. The curtain falls. The curtain rises a few minutes later.

SCENE 4

> The set is exactly the same as for the first part, except that over the back door is now a

number 4. The beginning of the scene is
played EXACTLY like the first time.

JEANNE gets up from the armchair and
goes toward the back door.

JEANNE

You're really too stupid. I'm going to go spend some money. I'm
asking one last time: Do you need anything?

GERARD

To be left alone.

She opens the door, leaves, slams it. Long
silence. Gérard turns around and gets ready
to go back to bed, then stops.

GERARD

I shouldn't be so harsh with her. I should trust her. That muscle
man next door, I'm sure he doesn't give a shit about her. I should
go lie down. I'm tired.

He crawls to his bed. The door opens. Jeanne enters,
holding herself against the wall. Gérard looks at her.

GERARD

You are back already? What's wrong?

JEANNE

I'm not feeling well. I can't breathe.

GERARD

Go, sit in your armchair! Can you do it?

JEANNE

Yes, it's gonna be OK.

> She goes to the armchair unsteadily and sits down.

GERARD

Stay calm. I will help you.

> He goes to her feet and with his teeth grabs the heels of her shoes and helps Jeanne take them off.

JEANNE

My medications? Where are my medications?

GERARD

They're on the table with the other ones, I suppose. You're scaring me.

> Jeanne looks through the bottles and finds the one she wants. She takes it, opens it. Her arm falls and all the pills spill on the floor. Gérard panics.

GERARD

Don't worry, I'll pick them up. How many do you need?

JEANNE

Three.

GERARD

Open your hand.

> He puts his mouth on the floor to pick the pills and brings them one at a time to Jeanne's hand.

GERARD

Make sure they don't fall. I'll get you some water.

> He goes to his bed and takes one of the
> bowls in his mouth and returns to the
> armchair. He puts the bowl on the floor.

GERARD

Take your pills. I have water for you. Put your hand in the bowl.

> Jeanne swallows her pills. Gérard takes the
> bowl in his mouth and lifts it as high as he
> can toward her hand. She dips her hand in
> the bowl and drinks the water from her
> fingers. Several times.

JEANNE

That's enough.

> Gérard puts the bowl as far away from the
> armchair as he can.

GERARD

Let me gather them. We shouldn't lose any.

> He goes behind the wall and returns with a
> dustpan in his mouth. He gathers the pills in
> a little pile. He puts the dustpan back.

GERARD

How do you feel?

JEANNE

Better. It will take a little longer. It's my fault. I forgot to take them this morning.

GERARD
(trying to crack a joke)
Sometimes, we panic for little nothings. Caress my head if you are strong enough.

She caresses his head.

JEANNE

Do you love me?

GERARD

I'll always love you, even after what...

JEANNE

Don't say another word. But will you ever forgive me one day?

GERARD

Never, never.
(looking down at his body)
But look at what you did to me. Look at my body! Look, look!

Jeanne looks away. The curtain falls.

A STORY IN THE SHAPE OF

a French song without music

TALONS AIGUILLES

Bruit fétichiste
Talons aiguilles
qui cliquent, qui claquent
Cliquetis érotique
Jimmy Choo, Monoprix,
Manolo, les 3 Suisses,
Louboutin, seconde main
Place Vendôme, rue Saint-Denis
Femme du monde, femme chic,
bourgeoise ou déesse
du trottoir, de la nuit
Cliquetis érotique
Place Vendôme, rue Saint-Denis
Fashion Week, maison close
Talons aiguilles
qui cliquent, qui claquent
Talons aiguilles
qui cliquent, qui claquent
Votre chanson me berce le cœur.
Vos talons me percent le cœur.

A STORY IN THE SHAPE OF

a novella

PIERRE GOES TO THE BIG CITY

1

Today, on his day off from a job that he feels will soon be replaced by a robot or shipped to China, Pierre got up really early, flossed twice, put on the clothes he had bought specifically for his trip to the Big City: khaki pants, pleated! The latest fashion! A crisp white cotton shirt, a striped tie, a navy blue blazer, and burgundy shoes that he lovingly buffed last night just before going to bed. He put them on the bedside table, next to the alarm clock, which he set at 4:30, so that they would be the first thing he would see when he woke up. And then, in the inside pocket of the blazer, he put what he calls his most beautiful fashion accessory: a brand-new credit card, his first ever, shiny and still unused, that he had ordered particularly for his trip to the Big City, because he had read in a magazine that the only people who use cashmoney in the Big City are tourists from small towns like his, and that people there look down on them. And so, he had put his credit card in the inside pocket of his blazer alongside the round-trip train ticket he had bought a week in advance, just to make sure that he would be able to get a window seat.

He arrived at the train station at 6:17 a.m., very early for the 6:53 train. It was on time and very crowded. Pierre wondered if those other people were going where he was going, but he decided that they couldn't be: they were not particularly well-dressed, and they didn't show any of the excitement that he himself had the hardest time hiding. So he figured that they were just going to another small town somewhere.

The train left at 6:53 sharp and arrived in the Big City's central station fourteen minutes later, at 7:07, right on schedule. It was Pierre's first trip aboard a supersonic train. To his surprise, everybody in the compartment got off, as he did.

2

PIERRE
(to himself)
Finally, I am in the Big City.

There is a big blinking sign that reads EXIT, and he approaches it, feeling like a million bucks! There is a huge opening in the wall and beyond it, a street! With sidewalks! With people, lots and lots of people! Walking! The sky is the most beautiful shade of chartreuse he has ever seen. The buildings along the street are so beautiful, all as shiny as his shoes, softly reflecting the sun! The air is fresh, very fresh, flowery but not sweet, just very oxygenistic. This must be a boulevard! And the people, they are so elegant, and they walk so lightly. No, they don't walk, rather they tiptoe. No, they don't tiptoe, they dance! They dance to the sound of the sweet, gentle music that fills the boulevard. It is beautiful music, much nicer than elevator music at the mall. I know that piece of music, Pierre, I have heard it before on the radio. I know that piece of music, but I cannot name it. It will come to me in a minute: Yes! It is George Gershwin, and the name of the piece is…why can't I remember it? "Walking the Dog," that's it! "Walking the Dog," Pierre. "Walking the Dog!"

Pierre doesn't know what to do. He is afraid to get on the sidewalk and start walking among these dancing people. They will notice he's not from here, and they will laugh at him. He thinks: Maybe I will just stay here and look at the beautiful people for awhile, and then I'll take the next supersonic train back to my small town.

But it was not meant to be. Somebody rushing from inside the train station bumps into him and pushes him onto the sidewalk. And there he is, in the middle of people who are dancing around him, getting so close but never touching him. He is terrified. He is trying to get back inside the train station, but there are too many people between him and the entrance. He thinks: I'll just get out of the way, and then I'll see what I can do. So he starts walking, or so he thinks. Because he's not walking, he's dancing, like everybody else, clumsily maybe, but dancing. Could he be a little bit like them? Look at you, Pierre, you can dance. And "Walking the Dog" keeps on playing, and everybody keeps on dancing. "Walking the Dog!" And Pierre dances, less clumsily already, and without noticing, turns the corner and leaves the boulevard. And he dances, but the music is rapidly getting fainter and fainter and, suddenly, it is gone. And Pierre doesn't dance anymore; he walks. And his new shoes are starting to hurt. And this street is not as nice as the boulevard. In fact, it's not nice at all. The buildings are dirty; the sidewalks are littered with trash; and the rare people are not the least elegant. A foamy goo is coming out of the sewers, filling the air with an unbearably acrid smell. And where did the music go?

Pierre turns back. He must return to the boulevard where the beautiful people are. He is sure that he came from that way. Or was it from the other side? You must pay more attention, Pierre! You are so easily distracted, Pierre! You are a daydreamer, Pierre! He tries to hear the music but nothing. And the sky is not that incredible shade of chartreuse anymore; it is grey, a dirty grey, a greasy grey. People are watching him. They don't look friendly.

PIERRE
(taking a deep breath)
Let's not panic!
I will find my way back to the boulevard.

He turns around and walks in that direction, but it is not the boulevard. From the corner of the street, he can see a piece of chartreuse sky that looks like the one above the boulevard. All he has to do is to walk toward it, and he will be back on the boulevard in no time. He feels so relieved.

He briskly follows the piece of chartreuse sky and starts whistling "Walking the Dog" like he has known that piece of music all his life.

3

It has been block after block of these dirty, sometimes boarded buildings. The acrid smell of the sewers is everywhere. But nothing looks like the boulevard. Pierre keeps on walking, ignoring the few people on the sidewalks. How long have you been walking, Pierre? And doesn't it seem like the piece of chartreuse sky is moving away from you faster than you are walking toward it? How are your feet, Pierre? You should have worn those shoes a couple of times before taking your trip to the Big City, Pierre, to break them in, like some people say. But you wanted them to be perfect, new, shiny, without a scratch, without any trace of having been worn, just like your new pants, and your new white cotton shirt that was so hard to iron, and your new blazer with your credit card and the train ticket in the inside pocket. The train ticket! The train, Pierre! You must get back to the boulevard, Pierre, because that's where the train station is, and you must get on the train to get back to your little town tonight, because you are working tomorrow and what would your boss say if you didn't show up for your shift? But your clothes are starting to smell like the sewers, Pierre. Will they let you on the supersonic train smelling like that, Pierre? But you must get on that train somehow. You cannot afford to miss that day at work, Pierre, because you need the money. You spent so much on those clothes and those shoes, and you will need every penny of that next check. Why is the piece of chartreuse sky moving away from you, Pierre? Are you walking too slowly? Can you hear the beautiful music? Can you see the boulevard in the horizon? Do you see anybody dancing? You have been walking for hours now, Pierre. Are you sure you are following the right piece of chartreuse sky? Look, on your left, behind your shoulder, there is another one. Doesn't it look brighter than the one you have been following, Pierre? And on your right, what about that one? Were they there all along? I don't remember seeing them before, Pierre. Are you sure you are following the right one, Pierre? Why are you following that one instead of the others, Pierre? The boulevard was never that far away! Why do you have to go through these dilapidated neighborhoods in your beautiful clothes, Pierre? The few people you pass on the sidewalk look at you funny, Pierre. Be careful. Pierre, I know the boulevard was never that far. You must be going in the wrong direction. You must be following the wrong piece of chartreuse sky, Pierre. What do you want to do, Pierre?

4

Pierre has followed every single piece of chartreuse sky all day long, going after one, then the other. There are now five or six of them, in different places, and they are always far away, and the blocks and blocks of dirty buildings and dirty sidewalks are starting to all look the same. But what is happening now, Pierre? The night is falling. Slowly. But it is falling. And the pieces of chartreuse sky are turning green, dark green and darker by the minute. Pierre, how will you know what direction to go now? A few streetlights are starting to come on, here and there, barely enough to see the ugly buildings, the ugly sidewalks, the foamy, acrid goo from the sewers, and the few people on the street. Where are you now, Pierre? Doesn't that smell make you nauseous?

5

Sounds! There are sounds coming from around the corner! Voices! Laughter! Happy sounds! This is not the boulevard. Pierre knows that much. But maybe, friendly people. They sound friendly enough. He goes to the corner, takes a deep breath, smiles, and turns. But it is not what he expected to see at all. That block is entirely made of one-story houses. A few people sit on chairs outside their doors, drinking beer, chatting with each other, and laughing loud. All the houses are exactly the same. Each of them has a huge metal cage on the right side, full of big, scary dogs that growl and bark the second they see Pierre. People come out of the houses and laugh at his horrified look. Somebody screams: "You're lost, Mister?"

Pierre turns around and walks away from those houses as fast as he can, almost jogging. The people laugh louder. They bang on the cages with metal bars, driving the dogs mad. Then, they open the cages and let the barking dogs chase Pierre who is running now as they are getting closer and closer to him. He gets to a tall, half-demolished stone wall that he manages to climb before the dogs get to him. The dogs' owners are having a wonderful time, watching him trying to escape the vicious animals.

As he runs away on the wall, it collapses behind him and lets a few dogs get closer to him. Pierre, watch your step. Don't stumble on the stones, Pierre! Don't fall, Pierre. Run faster! The dogs are closing up on you, Pierre. The wall is getting higher and higher. Pierre keeps on running as the wall collapses behind him. He is now at the very end of the wall with dogs ever closer to him. Pierre! No!

At that moment, he hears a voice: "Sir!"

He turns around. Firefighters! Holding a tarp! "Jump," they say. "Jump, sir!" Pierre looks at the firefighters, at the tarp, at the dogs about to attack him. He jumps. But nobody is holding the tarp. The firefighters are gone, if they ever were there. And Pierre crashes on the ground, on the tarp, and dies. And that is the end of Pierre's trip to the Big City. And the saddest part is: He didn't even get a chance to use his shiny, new, virgin credit card.

A STORY IN THE SHAPE OF

a screenplay

A JOB

THE WHOLE MOVIE IS SHOT WITH CELL PHONES AND DIGITAL CAMERAS, THE FIRST PART OF THE MOVIE FROM INSIDE A VAN. EXCEPT FOR THE PERSON BEING FOLLOWED, THE ACTORS ARE NEVER SEEN, ONLY PART OF THEIR LEGS, OR A SHOULDER, OR THE BACK OF ONE'S HEAD. THEY ARE REFERRED TO AS ONE, TWO, AND THREE.

BLACK SCREEN – PHONE CAMERAS TURN ON – OPENING CREDITS

> THREE (V.O.)
> This is going to be an easy buck, guys. A few bullets and we're going to be rich.

> TWO (V.O.)
> (laughing)
> Yes, for a week!

> THREE (V.O.)
> A week's pay for one hour of work is good enough for me. Let's not be greedy, please! Really! We sit here, in the comfort of our van, waiting for somebody to get out of a house. We follow him, we shoot him dead. We get paid. I would hardly call it work!

They all laugh.

TWO (V.O.)
Too bad this job doesn't come with a pension plan!

THREE (V.O.)
Or a Christmas bonus!

They all laugh.

ONE (V.O.)
All phones charged?

THREE (V.O.)
Check!

ONE (V.O.)
Cameras?

TWO (V.O.)
Check! Ready to kill!

They all laugh.

ONE (V.O.)
We're going to need proof of this, man! I don't want to have to bring that guy's head to the boss in a bucket of brine! This is not a spaghetti western!

TWO (V.O.)
This is the 21st Century, after all.

THREE (V.O.)
Technology is our friend!

They all laugh.

THREE (V.O.)
Here he comes.

ONE (V.O.)
Get going!

TWO (V.O.)
Camera! Action! Go!

INT. – VAN – DAY

ONE PHONE CAMERA IS TURNED ON, AND THE IMAGE IS
ON A SMALL PART OF THE SCREEN. WHEN DIFFERENT
PHONES OR CAMERAS ARE USED, THE IMAGES CHANGE
LOCATIONS ON THE SCREEN. NO ADJUSTMENT OF
COLOR, FOCUS OR ANYTHING ELSE. EVERYTHING IS
VERY ROUGH, VERY RAW. THE IMAGES TREMBLE, THE
WAY THEY COME OUT OF A CELL PHONE OR A DIGITAL
CAMERA, UNTOUCHED.

THE NEIGHBORHOOD IS VERY DETROIT-ISH, A
BOARDED HOUSE HERE AND THERE, AN EMPTY LOT
HERE AND THERE, A MANICURED LAWN HERE AND
THERE, BUT MOSTLY BORING, UNINSPIRED, REPETITIVE
EARLY 20TH CENTURY BRICK HOUSES.

A man has just left a house, a few houses from where the van is
parked. He drops a trash bag in the trash can on the side of the
house. He looks to his left and to his right, checks things around
him, goes to the sidewalk, then turns right, and starts walking away
from the house, away from the van. When he turns around the
corner, the driver of the van (One) turns on the ignition and drives
slowly in the man's direction.

BLACK SCREEN

TWO (V.O.)
I wonder where he's going?

THREE (V.O.)
To the morgue!

                    TWO (V.O.)
      To hell!

They all laugh.

INT. – VAN – DAY

THE STREET THEY'RE ON NOW IS WORSE THAN THE
LAST ONE. BURNED-OUT HOUSES, STRIPPED HOUSES,
BOARDED-UP HOUSES, TRASH EVERYWHERE.

The van follows the man from a distance.

                    ONE (V.O.)
      Well, I guess we don't have to worry about waking up the
      neighbors!

They all laugh.

The man stops in front of a tree, unzips his pants, and pisses
against it.

                    THREE (V.O.)
      Isn't it funny? All men do that. They always piss against a
      tree. It must be in the genes.

                    TWO (V.O.)
      The last piss!

                    ONE (V.O.)
      The last meal of the condemned!

                    THREE (V.O.)
      The last cigarette!

                    TWO (V.O.)
      The last supper!

They all laugh.

The man zips up his pants and continues walking. But suddenly he realizes he is being followed. He turns and looks at the van. He walks faster, looking over his shoulder with panic in his eyes.

> ONE (V.O.)
> Let's not wait too long! The bastard knows we're following him.

The man walks faster and faster, reaches an abandoned factory building, and runs around the corner to try to escape. The windows of the van go down. Shots are fired. The man collapses on the ground.

EXT. – STREET IN FRONT OF ABANDONED FACTORY – DAY

One, Two, and Three get out of the van and point their phones at the man on the ground. More shots are fired, so they're certain he's dead. They film what can now be officially called a corpse. Only feet and parts of legs around him are visible.

> THREE (V.O.)
> Great job! Give me the cashmoney!

One of the phones rings.

> ONE (V.O.)
> Perfect timing, boss. We just finished him.

> VOICE (O.S.)
> What the fuck are you talking about? Where are you? We got him.

> ONE (V.O.)
> But we just killed him!

                    VOICE (O.S.)
                (a sweet voice, laughing)
        You just killed the wrong guy, silly boy.

                    ONE (V.O.)
        Merde!

                    VOICE (O.S.)
                 (laughing again)
        No big deal! Where did you go?

                    ONE (V.O.)
        Where you told us: 9,735 on 1,834th Street.

                    VOICE (O.S.)
        No, idiot! 1,834 on 9,735th Street.

                    ONE (V.O.)
        Oops! My mistake.

                    VOICE (O.S.)
        Don't sweat over it!

                    ONE (V.O.)
                (to Two and Three)
        Let's get out of here. Wrong guy!

                    TWO (V.O.)
        Damn!

                    THREE (V.O.)
        What a waste of bullets!

BLACK SCREEN – PHONE CAMERAS OFF – FINAL
CREDITS

One, Two, and Three get into the van. They slam the doors, and
the driver turns on the ignition. The van leaves.

THREE

I wonder who he was. (panic in his voice) What about the cashmoney?

One and Two laugh.

THREE (V.O.)

Man, my rent is due tomorrow!

One and Two laugh.

ONE (V.O.)

You'll just have to get a job!

THREE (V.O.)

Yeah, right!

They all laugh.

A STORY IN THE SHAPE OF

a song without music

MY BEAUTIFUL AK-47

If you gave me an AK-47,
I would always love you.
If you gave me an AK-47,
I would go for walks with you.
If you gave me an AK-47,
I would be nice to your friends.
Oh, Grandma, you gave me
a revolver for my tenth birthday.
But Grandma, I'm a big boy now,
and for my thirteenth birthday,
all I want is an AK-47.
Grandma, dear Grandma,
I know you love me so much.
Oh, dear Grandma,
my favorite grandma,
if you gave me an AK-47,
I'd love you even more.
BUT! BUT! BUT!
If you don't give me an AK-47,
I'll tell your friends that you
steal cat food from
the convenience store.

A STORY IN THE SHAPE OF

a screenplay

THE RED DRESS

ON THE BLANK SCREEN: DAY ONE. BUT OF COURSE, IT'S NEVER DAY ONE.

INT. – ELEGANT TAXIDERMY SHOP – DAY

VERY CLEAN, VERY BRIGHT. A LARGE WINDOW ON EACH SIDE OF THE FRONT DOOR, BRINGING A LOT OF LIGHT AND ALSO GIVING PASSERS-BY A COMPLETE VIEW OF THE STORE. THE ANIMALS DISPLAYED IN VERY TASTEFULLY. NO CLUTTER. AGAINST THE BACK WALL IS A FULL-LENGTH MIRROR, BEHIND A LOW TABLE WITH A COMFORTABLE LEATHER ARMCHAIR ON EACH SIDE. ON THE LOW TABLE IS A BOX OF TISSUES, LIKE AT FUNERAL HOMES. THIS IS, AFTER ALL, A FUNERAL HOME OF SORTS. TEA OR COFFEE IS SERVED TO THE CUSTOMERS WHO BRING THEIR DEAD ANIMALS OR SIMPLY BROWSE FOR ONE IN STOCK. CHARLES, THE OWNER, IS VERY PROUD OF HIS SHOP AND HIS TRADE, AND IT SHOWS. ON EACH CORNER OF THE BACK WALL IS A DOOR. ONE GOES TO THE APARTMENT, THE OTHER TO THE LABORATORY/OFFICE. ON ONE SIDE OF THE STORE IS THE COUNTER, ALL MADE OF MAHOGANY, VERY DISCREET, NO CASH MACHINE HERE. INSIDE ARE CARDBOARD BOXES AND LOTS, LOTS OF TISSUE PAPER.

CHARLES, in his mid-fifties, coat and tie, very well-dressed and impeccably groomed with a Cary Grant-ish posture, stands in the middle of exotic animals and tropical birds, stuffed, of course. He looks at his watch, looks at the street. He takes a feather duster from behind the counter and dusts the animals.

CHARLES
(dusting a bird)
Feathers against feathers…

Again, he looks at his watch and at the street. He lovingly caresses a zebra.

CHARLES
Dead, and yet so beautiful…

He moves, ever so carefully, a few small animals in the window an inch or so, turns them a little, switches them, dusts them, all along keeping an eye on the sidewalk across the street and looking at his watch every ten seconds. Suddenly, his worried expression turns into a smile.

LARA, about thirty-five, appears on the opposite sidewalk. She wears an elegant red dress, but it is the only thing elegant about her. She is beautiful but a little vulgar: the BIG hair, the cheap oversized jewelry, the way she carries her bag, the way she walks, the way she chews gum. Charles looks at her with that childish smile of his.

CHARLES
Finally! Where were you?

He looks at his watch.

CHARLES
You are late. I was starting to be worried. You are eleven minutes late. It never happens.

He looks at her, relieved. He likes the way she walks, the way she puts her hand in her hair to fix it. He turns around and talks in the direction of the door to the apartment. His voice is warm, caring, the voice one has when talking to somebody one loves and has known for a long time.

>   CHARLES
> My love, I'm closing the shop. I'm going for a coffee and a little walk. I won't be late, I promise. I just need some fresh air. It gets so stuffy in here.

He doesn't wait for an answer. He looks at himself in the mirror, checks his teeth, uses some spray mouthwash, adjusts his tie, combs his hair, rubs the top of his shoes against the back of his pants, and checks his nails. He takes his wallet from his coat pocket to see how much money he has, goes to the counter and removes a couple of bills from a drawer and puts them in the wallet. The wallet goes back in his pocket. He leaves the light on. He locks the door and rushes across the street.

EXT. – SIDEWALK ACROSS FROM THE SHOP – DAY

THERE ARE BUSINESSES AS ELEGANT AS CHARLES'S SHOP. THE SIDEWALK IS QUIET; FEW PEOPLE ARE OUT TODAY.

Charles follows Lara from a distance. He cannot keep his eyes from her. Lara and her red dresses! Lara feels his presence, his eyes looking at her. She takes a small mirror from her bag, pretending to check her makeup. She can see Charles following her. He is far behind her, so that it wouldn't look like he's following her. The same routine happens every day, but she cannot get used to it. She turns the corner onto a street much less elegant. She looks straight ahead, ignoring windows and noises. She keeps on walking a block or so, with Charles still following her from a distance, until she gets to the bar where she works.

INT. – DILAPIDATED BAR – DAY

THE BAR HAS SEEN MUCH BETTER DAYS AND A MUCH LARGER CLIENTELE. THE STOOLS AROUND THE BAR HAVE RIPPED RED VINYL SEATS. ONLY THREE

CUSTOMERS ARE SEATED AT THE BAR, IN A GROUP. THE PLACE CERTAINLY COULD USE A GOOD COAT OF PAINT. ON THE WALL, SOME YELLOWED, OLD PICTURES OF ACTORS AND SPORTS FIGURES, AND TWENTY-YEAR-OLD ADVERTISEMENT MIRRORS FOR BEER BRANDS ARE THE ONLY DECORATIONS. JUST A REGULAR DUMP THAT USED TO BE A NICE PLACE IN THE FIFTIES AND SIXTIES, AS THE MODERN DECOR ATTESTS, TURQUOISE FORMICA AND ALL.

Lara walks into the bar. MARY, a woman in her forties, who has seen it all, tends bar. For her, every day is casual Friday, very casual Friday. Mary, the waitress from the shift before Lara's, washes glasses, not paying a bit of attention to JACK, CHUCK, and BUTCH, the three happy hour regulars. Three normal neighborhood drunks, like every neighborhood bar has.

> LARA
> Mary, I'm sorry to be late. Something came up.

> MARY
> (who hadn't noticed her)
> No problemo, Lara! Ten minutes! Don't worry about it. I have nothing planned for the rest of the day. Nothing! Plus, I had these gentlemen, these real gentlemen to keep me company.

Jack turns around and looks for gentlemen in the bar, under the stools, and gets up to look behind the counter.

> JACK
> (pretending to be perplexed)
> Gentlemen? Real gentlemen? Who could she be talking about? I don't see no gentlemen.

Everybody laughs. Mary looks outside.

MARY

Ah! And of course, like every day, here is Mister Charles.
He scares me, that man, with his tie and his attitude.

Lara looks at her, upset.

LARA

He's eccentric, that's all. Everything seems to scare you,
anyway. Well, you can go now. Thank you so much.

MARY
(under her breath)
Nothing scares me but Mister Charles, Mister coat and tie
and shiny shoes.

Charles walks into the bar. He doesn't say a word. He looks so out
of place. Mary catches the way Charles looks at Lara, smiles at
Lara, with Lara trying to look natural and professional.

MARY
(to Lara who gets upset)
No rush. I told you I have nothing better to do tonight. I'll
just stick around for awhile. Be on the other side of the bar
for a change. Lara, let me have a cognac.

Lara looks at her with a dirty look and brings her the cognac.

LARA

Enjoy!

The three customers look at Charles. He takes a handkerchief from
his pocket and uses it to dust the stool on which he is about to sit.

LARA
Good afternoon. Mister Charles. A coffee, as usual?

CHARLES

Please, forget the Mister, Lara. I've asked you a hundred
times: Simply call me Charles. A coffee, yes, as usual.

The other customers and Mary look at Charles. Lara fixes his
coffee. Charles looks at Lara and doesn't even see the other people
in the bar. Lara brings him his coffee. Mary looks at Lara and then
at Charles and doesn't like what she sees.

CHARLES

Your dress is beautiful. Red looks great on you. You should
wear only that color.

LARA

It's the same one as yesterday.

CHARLES

Why two days in a row? You have so many red dresses.

Mary looks at both Lara and Charles.

LARA

It's my favorite. I would wear it every day.

Charles, enthralled, looks at Lara and smiles with that childish
smile. The intensity of his stare makes Lara uncomfortable. She
tries to avoid it. She washes a glass, puts it back where it belongs,
and looks at the people on the sidewalk passing the bar. She
doesn't look at Mary either. It's the first time that Mary has ever
stayed in the bar more than a few minutes after Lara arrived.
Usually she leaves the bar at about the same time that Charles
walks in. But today, she's not about to move from her observatory.
Mary looks at Charles, then at Lara and the customers and doesn't
say a word. She looks at Charles again. Jack looks at Mary looking
at Charles. Lara accidentally looks at Jack, turns and looks at
Mary. Mary feels that Lara is looking at her and turns toward her.

LARA (V.O.)

But what is Mary doing here? Why isn't she going home? She is so nosy!

Charles is unaware of the things happening around him. He looks at Lara intensely while slowly sipping his coffee, smiling. When he's done, he puts his coffee cup down, wipes him mouth with the napkin that came with the coffee, takes out his wallet, pulls out a fifty dollar bill, and puts it on the counter next to the cup.

CHARLES

Keep the change, Lara. I will see you tomorrow. Have a good evening. The coffee was delicious, as usual.

LARA

Thank you, Mister Charles. See you tomorrow at the same time.

Charles doesn't even look at Mary or at the other clients. He looks at Lara. He leaves. He looks at her one last time from the sidewalk and then walks away. Everything is too quiet in the bar. Mary looks at the fifty dollar bill. The three customers look the other way. Lara grabs the money and puts it in her bra.

MARY

Ah! That explains a lot of things, a lot of things. Lara, please be careful. I don't like that man at all. He gives me the creeps. He always did.

DICK

And of top of it, Monsieur is a taxidermist, a stuffer, in case you don't know.

BUTCH

He's going to kidnap our poor little Lara and stuff her.

JACK

And he'll put her in his window for Valentine's Day!

The three guys laugh.

                    LARA
          (really upset and growing impatient)
You are so dumb, the three of you! Plus it's my business,
not yours, so shut up!

                    MARY
Stop, you Three Screwges! Or I'll ask him to stuff your
balls for Christmas, if you have any. It will be a nice
Christmas gift from me!

                    JACK
It seems we have upset those ladies. We must calm the
Valkyries, gentlemen. Lara, a round for everybody present:
Real gentlemen and Valkyries.

                    MARY
I'll have a cognac, an expensive one.

                    LARA
Me too. We might as well start the evening out right.

Lara fills the glasses, the usual for the Three Screwges, cognac for
the Valkyries, and distributes them. She grabs hers and empties it
in one gulp.

                    LARA
Thank you for the drink, I feel better already.

                    MARY
First of all, how do you know he's a stuffer? Did he tell you
himself? Or did you deduct it from his looks and behavior?

The Three Screwges laugh.

BUTCH

Very funny, Mary. Ask Lara. She knows Mister Charles very well. Don't you, Lara?

Lara is not amused. She pours herself another cognac and swallows it.

DICK

His store is, I'd say, about five minutes from here. By foot! Is it correct, Lara?

JACK

It's beautiful, very chic, very classy.

DICK

Very continental.

The Three Screwges laugh.

BUTCH

But it feels like death. It looks like death.

Nobody laughs.

LARA

Stop it right now or I'll throw you out! Enough!

INT. – TAXIDERMY SHOP – DUSK

IS SOMEBODY WATCHING THE SIDEWALK ACROSS FROM THE SHOP?

Charles is across the street from his shop. He looks inside from the sidewalk. He starts crossing the street, then turns around, gets back on the sidewalk, and walks away.

EXT. – DIFFERENT STREETS – DUSK

DIFFERENT STREETS, SOME MORE RESIDENTIAL, SOME MORE COMMERCIAL

Charles walks without a precise destination. Just to walk. He passes all kinds of people, including couples who seem in love. Those, he watches for a long time, sometimes following them for an instant. He takes his time.

> NARRATOR (V.O.)
> (not one of the actors)
> Charles pays attention to everything he sees, to everything he breathes, to everything he smells, to everything he touches. The roughness of bricks, the smooth and worn aspect of stones, the artificial sensation of cement or tarmac, the smell of the streets, the conversation of the people he passes, the way they are dressed, the way they look at him or ignore him. The noise of cars, the honking horns. The specific sound of bus doors when they open or close. He looks at the window displays, here and there. After all, it's like his windows with his stuffed animals. Either it interests you, or frankly, you don't care or even you dislike them. That's the way it is. To each his own. He thinks about the couples who looked at those windows together. He thinks about couples kissing. He thinks about the smiles, the laughs, those looks full of love or full of contempt, full of hatred sometimes. He thinks about people declaring their love, about the fights, the screams, the tears. He thinks about the people who, like him, take their walks by themselves.

Charles passes an art gallery having a show opening. He then turns around, looks at the painting in the window, and decides to walk in. The gallery is overcrowded. He picks a glass of wine. He tries to look at the paintings, but the place is too busy. Suddenly his nostrils flare. Charles freezes.

CHARLES (V.O.)
The smell of death! Who is it? I must find out.

He looks around, tries to locate the origin of the smell, but the gallery is too crowded. So he walks out, stands next to the door, and waits for people to leave. He tries to catch their smell as they leave. It is none of the first people. But, suddenly, here is the source of the smell: a couple in their sixties, ANN and PATRICK, bourgeois bohemians. They hold hands and are obviously happy to be together. Charles walks behind them, the way he walks behind Lara, but he stays close enough to be able to recognize their smell. He looks at them with curiosity and affection. They seem so happy.

CHARLES (V.O.)
Which one is it? Which one will die tonight?

PATRICK
Ann, tell me that you are hungry. I am famished.

ANN
Patrick, you are always hungry! But no fast food tonight, OK? It's not good for you. What did you think of the paintings? And the movie this afternoon?

PATRICK
I didn't understand the movie at all.

ANN
I'm not surprised. You fell asleep in the middle of it. And it's not the first time, by the way.

PATRICK
Why didn't you wake me up?

ANN

I did, when you started snoring. And that's not the first
time it happens either.

Patrick kisses Ann.

PATRICK

What would I do without you?

ANN

And me without you?

Ann and Patrick stop in front of a restaurant and read the menu in
the window. Charles becomes emotional.

PATRICK

Why don't we eat here? It was delicious last time,
remember? And it's not crowded at all. Fish OK with you?

ANN

Perfect!

INT – RESTAURANT – NIGHT

Ann and Patrick enter the restaurant. Charles follows them and sits
down at the next table. They order a martini. Charles orders a
martini. He looks at them intensely but as discreetly as possible.
Ann and Patrick hold hands and smile at each other, take their
time, sip on their drinks. They haven't even noticed Charles. They
order a glass of white wine; Charles orders a glass of white wine.
They order the poached salmon; Charles orders the poached
salmon. The white wine is served.

CHARLES (V.O.)

It's him. I clearly can smell it now. I'd love to hold up
my glass and say: "Cheers!" one last time. Poor man, if he
only knew! And her, what will she do?

Ann and Patrick's salmon is served. They get ready to eat. Charles's salmon is served. Charles has a sip of wine. Suddenly, Patrick holds his chest and collapses on the table. Charles sips his wine and starts on his salmon.

ANN

Patrick, Patrick!

She stands up, tries to get him off the table. But she is too weak.

THE MANAGER, a beefy guy, comes to the table and helps her put Patrick in his chair.

THE MANAGER (V.O.)
Why does it always happen to me?

THE MANAGER
I will call an ambulance.

He returns to the counter and calls. The waiters and the other customers act like nothing happened.

CHARLES
Miss, it's too late. He's dead.

ANN
(turning to Charles)
You are a monster! (turning back to Patrick) Patrick, my love!

Charles finishes his wine, grabs his plate, and goes to the counter.

CHARLES
The check and a doggy bag, please. The salmon is delicious. Could you put a few napkins in the bag? Thank you.

EXT. – SIDEWALK ACROSS FROM THE RESTAURANT – NIGHT

Charles nibbles at his salmon and looks at the restaurant. Things are not going well. Ann has lost it. She screams hysterically. The manager tries to quiet her down. The other customers and the rest of the staff pretend to ignore the mayhem and go about their business. The ambulance arrives. The medics walk into the restaurant with a stretcher, put Patrick on it, and take him to the ambulance. Ann follows them, screaming. Charles keeps on nibbling at his salmon. The ambulance takes Ann and Patrick to the hospital.

> CHARLES (V.O.)
> People never listen to me. I know he's dead. I could smell his death. Poor woman.

He finishes his salmon, wipes his mouth, and cleans his hands with a napkin. He throws everything in a trash can and walks away. He cries, looks around him, walks back home.

INT – TAXIDERMY SHOP – NIGHT

Charles enters his shop, locks the front door. He walks around the shop, looks at each and every animal. He touches them for a second and cries. He goes to the door to the apartment. Turns on the apartment lights and turns off the shop lights.

> CHARLES
> Good night, my little angels.

INT – KITCHEN – NIGHT

THE KITCHEN IS NEITHER NEW NOR OLD. EVERYTHING IS VERY CLEAN, VERY ORGANIZED. NO DISHES LYING IN THE SINK HERE. ON THE TABLE, NOTHING BUT A MAGAZINE. IN THE BACK OF THE ROOM IS A WHEELCHAIR, WITH SOMETHING IN IT COVERED WITH A CRISP CLEAN WHITE SHEET.

Charles walks to the wheelchair and removes the sheet. In the wheelchair, a woman, VANESSA, taxidermied, looking very much like Lara, except that her hair is shorter, closer to the face. She wears a red dress, very similar to the one that Lara was wearing. Charles puts the sheet on the chair next to the chair, grabs a feather duster, and starts to tenderly dust the corpse.

                    CHARLES
     And how are you, Vanessa my love, my beautiful wife?
     Did you miss me? I think I'll have a glass of wine. Would
     you like to join me? How was your evening?

He puts the duster down on the chair on top of the sheet, takes a glass from a cupboard, puts it on the table, goes to the wine rack on the counter, looks through the bottles, trying to decide which one he wants to drink.

                    CHARLES
              (as if answering her question)
     Mine? The usual. I went for my coffee, then for a walk.
     The streets were not too busy tonight. Then I bumped into
     an art gallery, a show opening, you know. I couldn't even
     look at the paintings; it was too crowded, so I got out of
     there.

He finds the wine he wants, goes to the table, pours a glass, puts the cork back on, and puts the bottle back in the wine rack.

                    CHARLES
     You want a sip? No?

He takes a sip.

                    CHARLES
     Then I went for dinner. Nice restaurant. Not crowded at all.

He takes another sip.

CHARLES
(answering another imaginary question)
What did I have? Poached salmon. It was delicious.

He has another sip.

CHARLES
I didn't want any dessert, so I finished my wine and left. It
wasn't expensive, either. All in all, pleasant. Let me come
and sit next to you for awhile.

He grabs a chair and his wine and goes sit next to her.

CHARLES
(looking at her)
We should go out from time to time. But you always want
to stay home. Don't you want to go see a movie at the
museum? How about a play? Or a concert at the
symphony? We used to buy season tickets, remember? And
the opera. Don't you miss going to the opera? They have a
good program this season; we should go. We need to do
more things together. I am tired tonight. I will go to bed in
a few minutes. You must be tired too. What time is it?

He looks at his watch.

CHARLES
10:56 already! Let me finish my wine, and we'll both go to
bed.

He finishes his wine, takes the glass to the sink, washes it, rinses it,
grabs a towel, and dries it. He then puts it back in the cupboard
from which he took it and puts it in the exact same spot. He goes
back to his wife.

CHARLES
Time to go to sleep. Good night, my love.

He takes the sheet and puts it over her. He goes to the back of the room and turns the light off.

CHARLES
(lovingly)
Good night.

ON THE BLANK SCREEN: DAY TWO

INT. – TAXIDERMY SHOP – DAY

It's 11:00. Charles is very busy. He carefully, professionally, obsessively wraps beautiful birds in layers after layers of tissue paper, depositing them in oversized boxes in a manner reminiscent of a religious ritual, and then, before closing the boxes, he fills every empty space with pastel Styrofoam peanuts. He does it very slowly, as if Robert Wilson was directing. He puts the boxes next to each other but does NOT put them on top of each other. While doing that.....

CHARLES
(in a soft, gentle and loving voice)
You are so beautiful, my beloved birds. Your feathers are so extraordinary, those different colors on each of them. And they are so soft, even in death. I will be so careful with you, my beautiful birds. Are you going to miss me the way I will miss you? And the other animals, are you going to miss them? They will miss you, you know. I would love to keep you all forever. But it is not the way it works. And tomorrow, more of you will go. I hate to see you go. It always makes me cry, always.

Charles puts a CD in the CD player hidden in the desk. The CD is of exotic birds singing in the forest, free. You can feel their freedom, their happiness. Their singing fills the shop. Charles leaves the desk and walks around the shop, caressing the animals, kissing them. He is crying. The shop door opens. Charles takes his handkerchief from his pocket and presses it against his eyes. He takes a deep breath, smiles a sad smile, and turns around. It's

MRS. MOREAU, an elegant forty-something woman who enters the shop.

> CHARLES
> Good morning, Mrs. Moreau. Please, sit down. Would you like a cup of tea?

She sits in one of the armchairs.

> MRS. MOREAU
> No, thank you.

> CHARLES
> A glass of port wine, perhaps?

> MRS. MOREAU
> Why not? If you join me. To celebrate Arthur coming home.

> CHARLES
> Let's.

Charles goes to the kitchen. Mrs. Moreau looks around her at the animals. The songs of birds keep on filling the shop. Charles returns, holding a small tray with two small crystal glasses half filled with port, and places it on the low table. He hands one glass to Mrs. Moreau and offers a toast.

> CHARLES
> (joyful, not at all forced or artificial)
> To the return of Arthur to his rightful home! Arthur is such a beautiful African grey.

> MRS. MOREAU
> To Arthur!

They both take a sip.

CHARLES
    Let me get him for you.

He puts his glass on the table and goes to the office. Mrs. Moreau
finishes her port. Charles comes back with Arthur the parrot
perched on a piece of branch resting on a wood stand.

                    MRS. MOREAU
                (excited, shedding tears)
    Arthur, my love.

She gets up and goes toward Charles.

                    CHARLES
    He's beautiful, isn't he? I really took extremely good care
    of him. I know you love him so much.

                    MRS. MOREAU
    Mister Charles, he is gorgeous. Just like when he was alive.
    You are so beautiful, Arthur.

She holds the bird in her arms very carefully, caresses him, kisses
him.

                    MRS. MOREAU
    Come, my love, we're going home. Mister Charles, I am so
    happy to have him back with me. I knew you would do a
    fabulous job. I gave your business card to all my friends. In
    fact, my friend Chantal Dutroit is coming to see you this
    afternoon. She needs your services. But let me pay you. A
    little more and I would have left without paying you. I am
    so happy.

The CD still plays. Mrs. Moreau takes a credit card from her wallet
and hands it to Charles.

MRS. MOREAU
And those bird songs are so beautiful. This place is so
serene.

She signs the credit cart receipt and puts the credit card back in her
wallet.

MRS. MOREAU
Come with Maman, Arthur!

CHARLES
Let me wrap him for you. You wouldn't want to damage
his beautiful feathers.

Charles takes a box from behind the desk and packs Arthur the
way he packed the other birds.

CHARLES
Would you like me to close the box?

MRS. MOREAU
Oh, no, he would suffocate!

Charles hands the box to Mrs. Moreau. She smiles at him and takes
the box. Charles goes to the door and holds it open for her. She
leaves and walks away from the shop. Charles watches her and
cries again. He finishes his glass of port, takes the tray and the
glasses back to the kitchen. He closes the door, walks to the office,
brings another bird to the desk, and starts wrapping it. The CD still
plays.

INT. – TAXIDERMY SHOP – DAY – A LITTLE LATER

Charles takes a board from a drawer. It says: "It's…I will be back
in an hour." He looks at his watch and writes in the empty space:
12:37. He goes to the apartment door and opens it.

CHARLES
My love, I'm going to the grocery store. I'll be back in less than an hour. Do you need anything?

He closes the kitchen door, goes to the desk to pick up the board, looks at his watch, and changes the 7 to an 8. He grabs the board, hangs it on the door, leaves, locks the door, turns left, and disappears.

INT. – TAXIDERMY SHOP – DAY – A LITTLE LATER

Charles returns from the grocery store, holding a few grocery bags. A baguette is sticking out from one of them. He locks the door and walks toward the kitchen. He opens the door, walks in, and closes it.

INT. – KITCHEN – DAY

Charles puts the bags on the kitchen table. He removes the sheet from Vanessa and dusts her with the feather duster. He then starts putting things away.

CHARLES
Vanessa, my love, you would not believe how busy the grocery store was. And the bakery too! You would think people have money to throw away. But I remembered to buy you a baguette. It is still warm, fresh like you like them. And some goat cheese, and some vegetables for a soup, and a steak and lettuce. And I didn't forget to buy eggs. Ha! However, I forgot to buy milk. No big deal, I'll go back tomorrow. And I bought some wine from the south of France. I think I'll have some. Would you like a sip, my love?

Charles gets a glass and the corkscrew, opens the bottle, pours some wine, and takes the glass to Vanessa. He brings it close to her lips but not touching them.

CHARLES
Cheers, my love.

He then puts the glass to his lips and takes a sip.

CHARLES
What time is it? 1:29. I only have nine minutes. I'll have a
piece of cheese. Would you like some cheese, my love?
Here, have a little piece!

He brings the cheese to her, close to her lips but not touching them.

CHARLES
Bon appétit!

He then eats the piece of cheese, finishes the glass of wine, takes a
bottle of mouthwash from the cupboard, gets a small crystal glass,
fills it with mouthwash. He rinses his mouth and gargles, spits the
mouthwash in the sink, rinses it, washes the glass, dries it, and puts
it back as well as the mouthwash where they came from. He puts
the cheese in the fridge and then covers Vanessa with the sheet.

CHARLES
I must go now! I'll see you in awhile.

INT. – TAXIDERMY SHOP – DAY

Charles comes out of the kitchen, looks back.

CHARLES
I'll be back soon, my love.

He closes the kitchen door, looks around, puts the bird songs back
on, grabs the duster, and starts dusting the birds.

INT. – TAXIDERMY SHOP – DAY – A LITTLE LATER

Charles wraps another bird.

CHARLES
The last one for this shipment…

He covers the bird with tons of tissue paper, adds some Styrofoam peanuts, closes the box, and tapes it. The front door opens. An elegant woman, CHANTAL DUTROIT, enters the shop and walks toward Charles.

CHANTAL DUTROIT
Are you Mister Charles?

CHARLES
Yes, good afternoon.

He takes the box he just closed and puts it next to the other ones, not on top.

CHANTAL DUTROIT
(nervously)
Good afternoon. My name is Chantal Dutroit. I am a friend of Mrs. Moreau. She suggested that I come to see you. Somebody has passed away.

CHARLES
Mrs. Moreau told me. Please accept my most sincere condolences. It is always extremely difficult, very painful. Do you have your friend with you?

CHANTAL DUTROIT
Yes, she is here.

Chantal Dutroit takes a small paper bag from her shoulder bag and gives it to Charles. He opens the bag and, inside, finds, to his horror, a mouse whose fur has been dyed pink.

CHARLES
Madame, please take back your mouse!

CHANTAL DUTROIT

It's my fault! What came to me to dye her hair pink? It's
what killed her, I'm sure. All these chemicals! But she
looked so pretty.

CHARLES
(losing it)

I cannot help you. I cannot stand mice. And think of the
damage these rodents could do in my shop! You must take
her back and leave now.

CHANTAL DUTROIT
(panicking)

But who will help me?

CHARLES

Look on the Internet. Goodbye, Madame.

He takes the bag with the mouse and shoves it in Chantal Dutroit's
shoulder bag.

CHANTAL DUTROIT

Mister Charles, you are not very helpful. I am very
distressed. What will happen to Bella?

CHARLES

Let me hold the door for you. I sincerely cannot help you.

CHANTAL DUTROIT

Bella! Bella! Nobody loves us.

Charles closes the door as soon as she leaves.

CHARLES
(screaming)

This is crazy! I'm going to make a sign that says: WE DO
NOT TAXIDERMY MICE. WE HAVE NEVER TAXIDERMIED MICE.
AND WE DO NOT PLAN TO TAXIDERMY MICE EVER. TAKE

YOUR DEAD MICE SOMEWHERE ELSE. PERIOD!

Charles goes to the apartment door, opens it, goes into the kitchen, and slams the door shut.

INT – KITCHEN – DAY – A LITTLE LATER

> CHARLES
> I think I'm going to have a drink. I'm shaking. My love, you will never guess what happened. People are crazy!

He uncovers Vanessa and dusts her. He takes a glass, fills it with wine, and takes a deep breath.

> CHARLES
> My love, would you like a sip? Let me tell you what happened.

INT. – TAXIDERMY SHOP – DAY – LATER

Charles looks at his watch. He moves around the shop, dusting animals and rearranging displays like he obviously does every day waiting for Lara to appear.

> CHARLES
> Almost 5:00.

He continues to kill time, like every afternoon. Looks at his watch again, steps to the window, looks at the sidewalk across the street. Lara appears in a different but very similar red dress. Charles smiles. He walks to the apartment door and opens it.

> CHARLES
> My love, I'm going for a cup of coffee and a walk. I won't be long; I promise.

He closes the apartment door, checks his wallet, his teeth, his tie, leaves the shop, locks the door, and crosses the street.

EXT. – SIDEWALK ACROSS THE STREET – DAY

Same routine: Charles follows Lara to the bar from the same
distance. As always, Lara knows that Charles follows her.

INT. – BAR – DAY

Mary is ready to leave. Lara walks in, goes straight to the bar, and
pours herself a beer.

                          LARA
            What happened to the Three Screwges?

                          MARY
           Haven't been here all day. Have fun. I got to run.

Charles enters the bar as Mary leaves. As always, he ignores her.
She gives him a dirty look. Lara finishes her beer and pours herself
a triple shot of cognac, and swallows at once. She is obviously
very nervous to be alone with Charles who looks at her with that
childish smile and doesn't pay any attention to her drinking.

                          LARA
        Good afternoon. Mister Charles. A coffee, as usual?

                          CHARLES
        Please, forget the Mister, Lara. I've asked you a hundred
        times: simply call me Charles. A coffee, yes, as usual. That
        dress looks beautiful on you. Red, always red, the best
        color for you.

Lara smiles and fixes Charles's coffee, brings it to him. As always,
she tries to avoid his stare. As always, she looks at the people on
the sidewalk. As always, Charles drinks his coffee very slowly,
looking at Lara. As always, when he's done, he takes a fifty dollar
bill from his wallet and puts it on the counter. But, since there is
nobody in the bar but the two of them...

CHARLES

Why don't you come a little earlier tomorrow? You could stop by the shop. I could show you around, tell you stories about my animals. We could have a sip of wine and chat for a few minutes. Tell me yes, please. Yes?

LARA

Maybe, maybe, but I cannot promise you anything. I am a very busy person.

CHARLES

I understand. But I hope that you will come, that you will find the time, fifteen minutes. I will be waiting for you. See you tomorrow.

LARA

See you tomorrow. And thank you for the tip, like usual.

Charles leaves the bar elated. Lara folds the fifty dollar bill and puts it in her bra.

EXT. – SIDEWALK ACROSS THE STREET FROM THE TAXIDERMY SHOP – DUSK

Charles looks lovingly at his shop, and then he suddenly panics.

CHARLES (V.O.)
I will have to wash, vacuum, and dust everything.

Charles turns away and goes for his walk.

NARRATOR (V.O.)
(not one of the actors)
Tonight Charles will not encounter the smell of death. He will not follow anybody because of it. He will just enjoy his walk, stop somewhere for an aperitif and a light dinner. And he will think about Lara and Vanessa, about Vanessa and Lara, about Lara and Vanessa.

ON THE BLANK SCREEN: DAY THREE.

INT. – TAXIDERMY SHOP – DAY

The sound of a vacuum cleaner comes from the kitchen. It stops.

> CHARLES (V.O.)
> Excuse me, my love, I'm going to vacuum under your
> chair. It will take but a second; don't be scared!

The vacuum starts again, then stops. The door to the kitchen opens.
Charles, wearing a pastel apron with ruffled edges, carries the
vacuum into the store, plugs it in, and start vacuuming. Then he
takes a cloth from his apron pocket and starts dusting. After
awhile...

> CHARLES
> What time is it? 3:47. I'd better get ready. It's as good as it
> will be.

Charles walks into the kitchen.

INT – KITCHEN – AFTERNOON

Vanessa is not covered with the sheet.

> CHARLES
> My love, I am going to put you in the bedroom for a little
> bit. You see, a friend of mine is coming in a few minutes
> for a glass of wine on her way to work. My love, she
> probably would not understand. It won't be long, my love, I
> promise you, and then, I'll bring you back here. You're not
> upset, are you, my love?

Charles pushes the wheelchair toward the bedroom door and bangs
it against a chair. One of Vanessa's eyes pops out and falls into her
lap. And a mouse escapes from the eye opening. Charles screams

in horror, runs after the mouse, and frantically tries to step on it but in vain.

CHARLES
(looking at Vanessa)
Don't worry, I will take care of it.

He starts going through the cupboards until he finds a container of mouse poison. He finds a small funnel that he inserts in Vanessa's open eye socket. He then pours the mouse poison into the funnel. When it is all in Vanessa's eye cavity, he removes the funnel and replaces the eyeball.

CHARLES
Better safe than sorry!

He returns to the cupboard and gets a stack of mouse poison packets that he opens and puts everywhere, including hidden places all over the shop. He returns to the kitchen.

CHARLES
It's getting late, my love. Let me take you to the bedroom.

And he does, just after covering her with the sheet. He comes back to the kitchen, gets the mouthwash from the cupboard, and does the mouthwash thing.

CHARLES
On second thought, due to all the excitement around here, I think I'll have a sip of wine, or maybe two.

He then pours a LARGE glass of wine and finishes it in a few gulps. Then does the wine glass washing routine.

CHARLES
Never a dull moment!

He looks at his watch and rushes back to the shop.

INT. – TAXIDERMY SHOP – AFTERNOON – A LITTLE
LATER

Charles grabs the feather duster and dusts away.

> CHARLES
> I wonder when she'll be here.

He looks at himself in the mirror. He's as nervous as a virgin
teenager in lust.

> CHARLES
> I should brush my teeth! And there is a spot on my tie. I
> must change it.

He puts his nose under his armpit, sniffs.

> CHARLES
> What time is it? 4:27! She'll be here soon.

He goes to the back room to change, comes back wearing a
different tie and jacket.

INT. – KITCHEN – MINUTES LATER

Charles stops in the kitchen and has a drink of wine directly from
the bottle. He returns to the shop.

INT. – TAXIDERMY SHOP – MINUTES LATER

Charles starts the routine of looking at his watch, moving the
animals an inch, and looking at the sidewalk across the street.

> CHARLES
> 4:47. What is she doing? We won't have time to chat. I'm
> going to have to rush her through the shop, and then it will
> be time for her to go to work. Where is she?

He goes to the pile of CDs in the desk and picks an opera compilation. Plays it full blast. And what is the aria about? About tragic love, about treason, of course. He listens to it crying, looking at the CD player. And then he turns around, looks at the sidewalk across the street, and sees Lara walking toward the bar without even looking at the shop. She's wearing a blue dress. Charles is horrified.

> CHARLES
> She's crazy! A blue dress? What is she thinking? I don't understand. What's happening? With all the red dresses I bought her. And she didn't even stop here. She didn't even look in this direction.

Charles walks around the shop, obviously upset. He rearranges the animals nervously, almost drops one. Tries to calm down.

> CHARLES
> Maybe she forgot. Or maybe she was late for her shift. But that blue dress! Horrible. I must go see her. I must talk to her. What came over her?

He makes sure that everything is in order in the shop. He goes to the kitchen, to the back door.

INT. – KITCHEN – LATE AFTERNOON

Charles puts Vanessa in her usual place in the kitchen. He lifts the sheet.

> CHARLES
> You see, my love, it wasn't too long. She couldn't make it today. She is so busy. It will have to be another day.

He puts the sheet back down, goes back to the shop.

INT. – TAXIDERMY SHOP – A FEW MINUTES LATER

Charles hesitates, walks in front of the mirror, goes through his routine of checking everything.

                    CHARLES
          My love, I'm going for a coffee and a walk. I won't be
          long.

He looks around, leaves, locks the door, crosses the street, and walks toward the bar. He is now frankly furious.

INT. – BAR – SAME AFTERNOON

Lara is by herself at the bar. She is swallowing beer like there is no tomorrow. The Three Screwges walk in.

                    BUTCH
          Good afternoon, Lara.

                    LARA
          Ah! The Asshole Brothers are back.

                    DICK
          She must have her period.

                    JACK
          Where is your boyfriend, Lara?

Lara is working on another beer. She takes a break to let go of a loud burp, then goes right back to drinking her beer, all smiles.

                    BUTCH
          This establishment is so classy.

The three of them sit down at their regular spot. Lara pours herself another beer.

JACK

And speaking of class, here is your boyfriend, Mister
Charles. Please, don't piss behind the bar; it might
displease him.

Lara serves them their usual.

LARA

But if I fart, it's OK?

They all laugh.

DICK

We love you when you're drunk.

Charles walks into the bar. The Three Screwges look away.
Charles doesn't say anything. Neither does Lara. She starts fixing
his coffee.

CHARLES
(very hateful voice)
A white wine, dry.

Lara leaves his coffee on the machine and pours him a glass of
white wine.

CHARLES

How much is it?

LARA

Five dollars.

CHARLES

Blue looks terrible on you. It makes you look older, much
older.

Charles takes a five dollar bill out of his wallet, puts it on the
counter. He finishes his wine and leaves without a word. No tip.

EXT. – SIDEWALK ACROSS FROM THE TAXIDERMY SHOP
– DUSK

Charles looks at the shop. He shrugs and goes on his walk.

EXT. – STREETS, SIDEWALKS, PEOPLE, CHARLES – DUSK

Charles stops at a street corner and inhales deeply. His nostrils are
flaring. The smell. He follows it. It's another couple, this time in
their late thirties, walking slowly, looking at displays in windows,
stopping for a kiss. The woman, HELEN, seems nervous,
preoccupied, vulnerable. The man, STEVE, is oblivious to her
tenseness. Charles walks behind them, again pretending not to
follow them. He is so good at it.

                    HELEN
        Let's go home. I'm cold.

                    STEVE
        If you want. What's wrong?

                    HELEN
        Nothing.

Charles continues to follow them.

                    NARRATOR (V.O.)
                (not one of the actors)
        Steve and Helen smile at each other, but Helen's smile is...
        Charles cannot find the word: sad, fake, a cry for help?

                    HELEN
        Go buy me a pack of cigarettes, please.

                    STEVE
        But you don't smoke!

HELEN

Please. I'm going home. I'll see you in a minute.

STEVE

You are crazy!

He enters a store to get some cigarettes, looks at some magazines, takes his time. He looks at Helen in the distance. Charles follows her. The smell is hers. Helen enters an apartment building. Charles follows her inside at a distance.

INT. – APARTMENT BUILDING – NIGHT

Helen unlocks the door of her apartment, enters, and locks the door from the inside. Steve enters the building and goes toward the apartment. Charles hides around a corner. There is a gunshot. Steve runs to the door of the apartment, tries to open it. He bangs on the door.

STEVE

Helen! Helen!

He drops the magazine and cigarettes, fumbles for his keys. He tries to force the door. He cries out her name like an animal.

CHARLES

Sir, it is no use. You need to call the police. She is dead, sir.

Steve keeps on banging on the door, screaming her name. He doesn't hear Charles. Charles shrugs and leaves.

ON THE BLANK SCREEN – DAY FOUR

INT. – TAXIDERMY SHOP – LATE AFTERNOON

It's the end of the afternoon. The shop is about to close. Charles looks at the sidewalk across the street.

> CHARLES
> That blue dress!

He looks at his watch. Lara appears on the sidewalk across the street. She wears a red dress. Charles smiles.

> CHARLES
> What's going on?

Lara almost falls. She can hardly stand.

> CHARLES
> She's drunk.

Lara walks erratically, laughs loudly, drops her bag, almost falls picking it up, and keeps on walking toward the bar. Charles quickly checks himself and shortens his routine, then stops.

> CHARLES
> No, I can't go. I don't want to see that. Drunk! At 5!

He grabs the feather duster from behind the counter and dusts the animals nervously. After a few seconds, he puts the duster back, stands in front of the mirror, checks himself again. Then he goes to the apartment door, enters the kitchen.

INT – KITCHEN – SAME AFTERNOON

Charles pours himself a glass of wine, drinks it in one gulp, grabs the mouthwash bottle, drinks some directly from the bottle, gargles, spits it into the sink, and leaves everything as it is. He then goes to the bathroom, takes a piss, flushes the toilet, and comes back to the kitchen, looks at his hands, goes to the kitchen sink, and washes them with dish-washing liquid.

> CHARLES
> Damn! She's gonna hurt herself.

He grabs the kitchen towel, dries his hands, and throws the towel on the table. He pours himself another glass of wine, and this time sips it slowly, trying to calm down. He looks at Vanessa, covered with the sheet. He finishes his wine.

CHARLES

My love, I'm going for a coffee and a little walk. I won't be long. I just need some fresh air.

He leaves the kitchen, closes the door.

INT – TAXIDERMY SHOP – MINUTES LATER

Charles takes a last look in the mirror in the shop, uses the spray mouthwash, goes outside, locks the door.

EXT – STREET – A SHORT TIME LATER
Charles crosses the street and walks toward the bar.

INT. – BAR – DUSK

Lara is drinking a beer. The Three Screwges are laughing. Mary is furious.

MARY

Lara, just go home. I'll take your shift. Look at you! And stop drinking!

Mary grabs the beer from Lara's hand and empties it into the sink.

MARY

Enough is enough!

Lara gets another glass and pours herself another beer. She starts drinking.

LARA

Nobody tells me what to do.

Mary gives up; the Three Screwges are having a ball; and Charles enters the bar. Everything stops; everybody freezes. Charles sniffs the air. The smell! The smell is here, in this room. He sits at his usual stool and looks at Lara, horrified this time.

LARA
So what, Mister Charles, you've never seen a drunk woman? Let me fix you a coffee.

CHARLES
It's not that at all.

Lara fixes his coffee, turns around toward him.

LARA
It cannot be my dress. It's red today, like you like it.

MARY
Forget his coffee! Go home and go to bed!

She looks at the Three Screwges.

MARY
I am sure one of these gentlemen will accompany you to your door, right?

The Three Screwges look the other way.

CHARLES
I will; it would be a pleasure.

Mary is not pleased, but since the Three Screwges are still looking the other way...

MARY
It's very nice of you, Mister Charles.

CHARLES
Are you ready? The fresh air will be good for you.

LARA
You keep your hands in your pockets, Buster!

They leave. Lara staggers. Charles watches her and tries to help her. She screams something. Charles puts his hands in his pockets sheepishly. Mary watches the two of them, then turns to the Three Screwges.

MARY

Lazy cowards!

EXT. – SIDEWALK – DUSK

Charles and Lara walk. Charles stops in front of his shop and looks inside from across the street.

NARRATOR (V.O.)
(not one of the actors)
The smell is hers indeed. Charles knows there is nothing he can do. But maybe yes, if he protects her, if he watches out for her.

They arrive at a bridge.

EXT – BRIDGE – DUSK

On the river beneath the bridge are a few boats. Lara laughs.

LARA
How about stopping somewhere for a drink?

CHARLES

Another day.

Lara steps on the railing of the bridge and decides to cross the bridge that way. Charles panics.

> CHARLES
> You are crazy; you will fall. Come down.

He tries to grab her.

> LARA
> You keep your hands in your pockets, Buster!

She laughs. She's not listening. Charles goes back to the beginning of the bridge, gets on the railing, and tries to get to Lara, but, before getting to her, he slips and falls into the river. Lara looks at him and laughs.

> LARA
> What an idiot! Don't worry. I'm coming to help you, Mister Charles.

A boat goes toward Charles to get him out of the water. Lara doesn't see the boat, gets ready to jump.

> CHARLES
> No, Lara, no!

Lara jumps from the bridge and crashes on the boat going toward Charles to rescue him. The people on the boat try to help Lara. A few more boats approach. Charles cries.

> CHARLES
> It's useless. You can see she's dead.

The people on the boat look at him, not believing what they hear.

> CHARLES
> I know she's dead.

EXT. – STREET IN FRONT OF TAXIDERMY SHOP – NIGHT

A police car stops in front of the shop. Charles gets out, his clothes drenched, a blanket over his shoulders. A POLICE OFFICER accompanies him to the front door.

> THE POLICE OFFICER
> Here we are. Good night, sir.

Charles finds his keys, enters the store, locks the door behind him, goes to the kitchen.

INT – KITCHEN – NIGHT

Charles looks at Vanessa without a word, goes to the bedroom, gets undressed and puts on a bathrobe. He returns to the kitchen, looks again at Vanessa, pours a glass of wine, takes a few sips, his eyes fixed on her. He puts the glass on the table, uncovers Vanessa, kneels in front of her and starts crying.

A STORY IN THE SHAPE OF

a song without music

IT CAN'T BE TRUE

It can't be true!
Yesterday,
you were OK.
Getting better,
right?
Getting well,
right?
But this morning,
my love, you
didn't wake up.
You died,
in the middle
of the night.
Your fingers,
the color of butter,
and so cold,
so cold already!
It can't be true!
I had fallen asleep,
missed your last moments.
It can't be true!
Of all times
to fall asleep!
It can't be true!
You were back home,
finally,
from the hospital.
A bed for you
in the living room
to look at the garden,

to watch the dog play.
It was to be you and me,
you and me again.
Together,
forever.
It can't be true!
After all this time
spent in that room,
that hospital room,
but you were home now.
It can't be true!
What did I miss?
Was I stupid?
Was I drunk?
It can't be true!
You were coming home
to die.
Did they tell me?
Did they?
It can't be true!

A STORY IN THE SHAPE OF

a painting

PORTRAIT II

How Giana regained her beauty after a motorcycle accident disfigured her

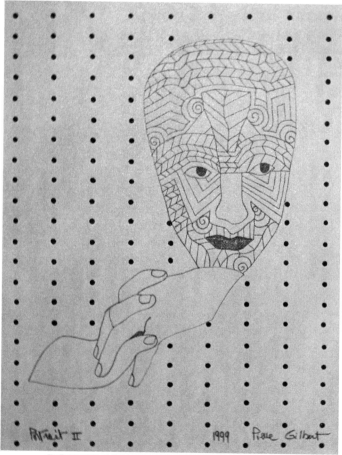

PORTRAIT II   Pierre Gilbert   1999

A STORY IN THE SHAPE OF

a novella

PIERRE'S VACATION

1

Pierre wakes up in an exceptionally good mood. He looks at the clock: 7:15. He sticks out his tongue at the clock, turns over, and goes back to sleep.

You see, it's Pierre's first day of his annual vacation, and he's planning to enjoy those precious two weeks to the max. He has organized every detail. He bought all the supplies he could ever need: toilet paper for a lifetime, paper towels, tissues, toothpaste, dental floss, hypoallergenic shampoo, soap, and bubble bath. Laundries are all done: everything is folded and put where it belongs. And the house is spic-and-span (well, almost): the CLEANING LADIES R US were here a few days ago and, man, are they ever good cleaners! And they don't break anything, and, even better, they don't steal anything, according to their brochure. The freezer and fridge are full. They are a work of art. They contain so many types of fresh or frozen meats and seafood – duck, rabbit, pheasant, some goat, some quails, salmon (fresh and smoked), trout (fresh and smoked), shrimp, etc. Of course, there is cheese, all French. Then, fruit and vegetables, some already cooked and in the freezer. Plus all the essentials, from milk to tofu. In the pantry, there are fourteen bottles of decent champagne (one for each day) and a sufficient supply of white, rosé, and red wine. It's interesting, don't you think, how rosés have a bad reputation.

Pierre is ready for his vacation! Cook, eat, and drink; see nobody, ignore the phone; read in bed most of the day, especially his favorite book: *The Fallacy of the Concept of Logic in Western Civilization;* take naps; and, of course, from time to time, masturbate. The curtains stay down, and Pierre stays home, naked, FOR TWO WEEKS! The perfect vacation. All planned.

Pierre wakes up, agitated.

PIERRE
The saffron! I forgot to buy saffron! What time is it? 9:25.
The store is open! I might as well go now.

He gets up, gets dressed, goes downstairs, and grabs a credit card and his keys. Pierre, do you really need to have saffron? I suppose you do: your saffron and garlic mayonnaise is to die for. And your bouillabaisse!

Pierre walks to the grocery store a few blocks from his house. He leaves through the back yard and turns to the right. The breeze brings him an unknown perfume, a scent dreams are made of, a combination of man's sweat and Chanel No. 5. He keeps on walking in the direction of the store, and the fragrance gets stronger and stronger, addictive, intoxicating. He passes a couple of backyards as manicured as his own. And, there, is the origin of the smell. A bush, six to seven feet tall, full of beautiful, huge, white flowers and luscious leaves, in the middle of which stands a naked man, all smiles.

> PIERRE
> Good morning, sir.
> Looks like another nice, warm, sunny day.
> Don't you think?

The man in the middle of the bush doesn't answer him, doesn't even notice him, and keeps on smiling. The bush's fragrance is deliciously overwhelming.

Pierre gets to the store and buys several bottles of saffron. In fact, he buys all the saffron they have in stock. All he can think about is the perfume of the flowers in that bush. Walking back, the scent is there again. It seems even stronger than before.

> PIERRE
> I'm gonna ask that man the name of that bush.
> It's strange; I don't remember seeing it before.

When he gets there, the naked man is gone; the bush is more gorgeous than before; and the smell is more intoxicating than ever. Pierre walks toward the bush. Pierre! Don't go into that backyard! It's trespassing, Pierre, and you shouldn't do that. But Pierre doesn't listen. He has to get to the bush. He has to pick a flower. Pierre, don't do that! You're not only trespassing, you're stealing. But Pierre cannot resist. The branch snaps; the flower is in his hand but only for a moment. Suddenly the flower and the whole bush turn to dust.

> PIERRE
> What have I done?

He looks around to make sure nobody saw him, especially not the naked man, and runs to his house. Oh, Pierre, there you go again! I told you not to pick that flower! And your finger is bleeding! Probably from when you snapped that branch! Why can't you leave things alone, Pierre? You always get in trouble, Pierre. And see what you did, Pierre? Now, the sweet scent is gone; nothing of it is left, Pierre.

Pierre returns to the house, washes his hands, and puts a bandage on his bleeding finger.

> PIERRE
> Great start for a vacation! Well, let's celebrate, anyway!
> Una copa de vino blanco, por favor.
> Even better, make it champagno!
> Vive les vacances!

Pierre gets naked, gets a bottle of champagne and his favorite champagne glass, brought back from France in the 1980s, the stem being a naked lady whose pointed tits leave a titillating feeling on the finger. The cork pops. The glass gets filled. Pierre has a sip.

> PIERRE
> I should get some cheese out of the fridge.
> Why didn't I think about it before?
> Well, it's only 10:35. What should I have for breakfast?

Everything tastes good with champagne.
How about a slice of prosciutto on an artichoke heart, braised:
the artichoke heart, not the prosciutto, it goes without saying;
with a splash of lemon and a crack of pepper?

Oh, Pierre, you love your food, don't you, which might explain your cute belly. But it's your vacation, Pierre, so you can do whaaaaaaaaaaaaaaaaaaaaaaaatever you want. Pierre nibbles at his prosciutto/artichoke breakfast, and for some reason, it tastes even better than usual. The prosciutto is sweeter; the artichoke is artichoker; and the pepper is pepperer. And the champagne is champagner, and the tits on the glass are titillatinger.

PIERRE
When you're on vacation, everything tastes better;
everything feels better; everything is better.

He pours another glass of champagne, sips it slowly.

PIERRE
Well, it is time to get back to that nap that was regrettably
interrupted by the saffron episode.

He puts the bottle in the fridge, and upstairs he goes.

2

It feels so good to be in bed. Pierre is ready for a good nap, but all he can think about is food and cooking. Try to go to sleep, Pierre. You just finished breakfast; you don't need any more food. That's why you're gaining weight, Pierre. But Pierre is hungry. He gets up, goes downstairs, opens the fridge, looks inside the freezer, and goes to the pantry.

PIERRE
Rabbit for lunch. And more champagne.
But first, I'd like a glass of water.

Pierre has his water, pours himself a glass of champagne, and gets the rabbit out the fridge. It is already cut into pieces. He gets the iron skillet from the pantry, puts it on the stove, and drops a big chunk of butter into it.

PIERRE
Maestro, please!

He goes to his computer, which is on the kitchen's countertop, and starts Purcell's "Dido and Aeneas."

PIERRE
Opera is better than sex! At least on the days
when you don't have anybody to have sex with!

The pieces of rabbit get covered with Dijon mustard. The gas is turned on; the butter is melting and now bubbling. There go the pieces of rabbit to be browned. And now, the potatoes for the mashed potatoes get peeled, cut in half, and thrown into water.

PIERRE
I'd better have nutmeg for the mashed potatoes!
Of course, I have nutmeg!
I don't want to have to have to back to the grocery store!

He goes to the pantry and finds the nutmeg.

PIERRE
I should cook more potatoes.
I might as well fix mashed potatoes for a few days.
And how about a soup?

Pierre gets super busy in the kitchen, cooking for what looks like weeks. He cannot stop. Leek soup. Pineapple and coconut clafouti. Poached salmon. Braised Belgian endives. The rabbit, the mashed potatoes. A goat stew. Shrimp. Flambéed apples. And the saffron garlic mayonnaise for the shrimp and for the bouillabaisse. The food is piling up. And Pierre feels very strange. His skin is making love to him. And he cannot stop touching it. While cleaning the Belgian endives, he caresses his shoulders. While slicing the pineapple, he caresses his stomach. While skinning the salmon, he caresses his thighs. While chopping the leeks, he kisses his own hands.

3

Lunch is ready! The table is set. Linen tablecloth covered with a gold-decorated sari. And a linen napkin. Pierre always says that nothing touches his lips but the best. The silverware is sterling; the china is white with a gold rim; and the crystal glasses have a similar gold rim. 1920-ish. Pierre pours a bowl of leek soup and sits at the dining room table. He lifts his champagne glass.

PIERRE
Cheers! And (imitating Julia Child) bon appétit!

The sip of champagne is so delightful. Pierre has his first spoonful of leek soup and starts to make ecstatic noises. Oh, Pierre! I know your leek soup is good, but it's not THAT good! And you don't have to make all these noises eating it! You don't have to caress your body as you eat either, Pierre. What is happening to you, Pierre?

Pierre finishes his bowl of soup, goes to the kitchen, pours some more, eats it, and goes back to the kitchen for another serving, eventually finishing the whole pot.

Pierre! Stop acting like a little boy. What are you going to do with the rest of the meal now that you have stuffed yourself with soup, Pierre? But Pierre is not finished eating. He puts the saffron and garlic mayonnaise in a fancy bowl, goes back to the table and, one by one, eats the half pound of shrimp, each dipped in his mayonnaise, still making those noises and still caressing himself. He finishes the champagne; he brings red wine and water to the table. Pierre, you are a pig today! Stop right now! You're gonna get sick! But Pierre continues eating, devouring the whole rabbit and three servings of mashed potatoes.

And since when do you drink so much water? You used to say: Water is for dogs. And you would quote Victor Hugo: "God only created water; man created wine."

Now, Pierre is having some goat stew. And an assortment of cheeses on crispy bread and then, half the pineapple and coconut clafouti. And always, those noises and caresses. At the end of dessert, he stands up and, with his head thrown backward, starts howling at the moon like a wolf, rubbing his nipples. Pierre! Stop it, you are scaring me! Stop it! Stop it! Stop it now!

4

Pierre is back in the kitchen, putting the dirty pots and pans in the dishwasher. He washes the china and crystal and puts them in the drainboard. His strange behavior continues. He prepares more food. He puts five big potatoes in the oven. Baked potatoes, indeed, to have with a slice of pâté, some cornichons, and a touch of lettuce, and butter mixed with chives put on top of the sliced-open potato. A chicken liver pâté or a rabbit pâté loaded with pistachios! They are waiting for you in the fridge, Pierre; you made them a few days ago, because they have to sit. And you took a special trip to the Polish butcher to buy their in-house cured bacon to line the pâté. Always the best for you, Pierre. Nothing from a can but caviar.

And talking of bacon, Pierre is starting a choucroute, duck fat and all. And there goes the rest of the bacon and all kinds of other meats. Pierre, a choucroute takes five hours before it's ready. Are you gonna cook all night? What's wrong with you? But he pours the white wine on the choucroute and turns on the heat under it. Choucroute, it is. Pierre reheats the poached salmon and the Belgian endives and prepares a little dessert snack: dried figs halved and stuffed with nuts dipped in honey. Just a small plateful.

Salmon and braised Belgian endives are a match made in heaven. Actually, any fish goes well with braised Belgian endives.

Pierre goes to the fridge, removes the pâtés, cuts a thick slice of each one, and puts them on a plate, and then fixes the chive/butter combination. Another glass of water, another sip of wine. Some more salmon and Belgian endives. Everything is cooking along.

Suddenly, he has to grab the countertop. He is getting very dizzy, and his body is sending him overwhelming signals. On his legs, buttocks, back, and chest are pointed things pushing on his skin from the inside. They are not painful, just extremely intense, extremely erotic, and, once again Pierre howls at the moon, this time in a very melodic way.

5

But now that "Dido and Aeneas" is finished, how about Cecilia Bartoli singing Vivaldi? Opera, champagne, and good food! Heaven on Earth! Pierre is hungry and doesn't want to wait for the baked potatoes, much less for the choucroute garnie! How about a little salad as a snack? Pierre gets a mixing bowl, throws in some lettuce and a few chopped shallots, goes to the pantry and gets the bottle of olive oil he loaded a week ago with tons of garlic and a million flowers of lavender. There goes the olive oil and a touch of date vinegar and some crumbled goat cheese. The perfect salad when you're hungry! And he is. He doesn't even bother putting it on a plate. He sits at the dining room table and eats it from the bowl.

The pointy things inside of him are getting bigger, pushing his skin further and further out. Pierre finishes his salad, picks up his linen napkin, and wipes his mouth. He can hardly make it back to the kitchen. He is getting dizzy again. He holds himself close to the fridge and starts howling again. The pointy things inside of him are now, one by one, piercing his skin and coming out. They are all pointing upward. No blood is shed. The sensation is not one of pain, but of orgasmic delight. Pierre faints and collapses to the floor.

6

Pierre wakes up, stands, and goes to the stove to make sure that nothing is burning. Ten minutes for the baked potatoes. He goes upstairs to look at himself in a full-length mirror and parades in front of it.

PIERRE
These little pointy things are…………cute.

He touches some of them, and it gives him a tingling sensation. A very nice tingling sensation indeed.

PIERRE
This could be a very nice vacation.

He goes downstairs and removes the potatoes from the oven, puts some sliced cornichon on top of the pâté, and adds a baked potato topped with a spoonful of chive butter. He takes his plate and his glass and goes to the dining room.

PIERRE
But what if I sit on the small pointy things
on my butt and crush them?

He turns around, goes back to the kitchen, puts his plate and glass on the countertop, and starts eating. Standing in front of the plate. Just like a normal person would do. But his obscene hunger is gone. He just sips red wine and nibbles.

7

Pierre! This is not a case of the zits. These little pointy things don't look healthy. And what if they get infected! You need to call your doctor. Or go to the emergency room. Pierre, I could swear these little pointy things are getting bigger. But Pierre just keeps on nibbling. Pierre! These little pointy things ARE getting bigger. And on each side of the little pointy things, there are now tiny, tiny, little pointy things, Pierre! Call 9-1-1! Pierre!

8

PIERRE
I'm not one to pat myself on the back,
but those pâtés are excellent.

I always say:
If you start with good ingredients and
cook them right, you get good food.
I pity the masses who feed on frozen dinners.

And Pierre keeps on nibbling away. He switches from Cecilia Bartoli to his favorite version of Rossini's "La Cenerentola." And after the overture and a few more sips of wine, he starts to sing along. Bad idea. But it is Pierre's vacation, and he does whatever he wants. Strangely enough, the little pointy things, getting bigger and wider, don't seem to stretch Pierre's skin around them. It almost looks like the little pointy things are feeding off Pierre's skin as they grow. And Pierre couldn't feel any happier. He dances along to the opera's music, caressing the little pointy things. Which are not little pointy things anymore for two reasons: One, they're not that small, and they are getting longer and fatter. Two, they are not straight and pointy anymore. They are getting curvy, going in all directions but down. But they feel so good to Pierre. As he dances (if you can call that dancing), he caresses the used-to-be-small-pointed-things and is in pure ecstasy. Another bottle of champagne is in order!

And through the night he dances, sings, and conducts the orchestra, sipping champagne, nibbling at food. He doesn't bother putting things in the fridge. And the branches coming out of him are growing bigger and bigger and are now covered with leaves.

At dawn, the bush that Pierre is carrying blooms, and their perfume fills the kitchen, a scent dreams are made of, a mix of Pierre's sweat and Chanel No 5. And Pierre wants to share it with the world. He steps out in his manicured yard and stands in the middle of it. An intense sensation fills his body. From the soles of his feet, roots grow. Pierre has never felt so happy. He would like to continue dancing, but his feet are now affixed to the ground.

PIERRE
I don't need to dance.
I am just fine where I am.
This scent is so extraordinary.

Little by little, Pierre is sucked up by the bush, his smiling face finally disappearing into the plant. And the flowers are getting bigger, and their bouquet more intoxicating. And the whole neighborhood can enjoy it.

That is, until somebody walks by, cannot resist, and picks one of the flowers.

CPSIA information can be obtained at www.ICGtesting.com
Printed in the USA
BVOW010009161012

303066BV00007B/41/P